OBERON'S MEATY MYSTERIES:

THE SQUIRREL ON THE TRAIN

OBERON'S MEATY MYSTERIES:

THE SQUIRREL ON THE TRAIN

Kevin Hearne

Subterranean Press 2017

First Edition

ISBN
978-1-59606-847-6

Subterranean Press
PO Box 190106
Burton, MI 48519

subterraneanpress.com

SQUIRREL, INTERRUPTED

I do not understand why humans tend to fear clowns more than squirrels. Atticus says it's probably all Stephen King's fault, which doesn't make much sense to me, but I'm sure he's right. That still doesn't explain why people are ignoring the mountains of evidence that squirrels have a sinister agenda and the ability—the agility!—to carry it out. They can climb trees and dang near anything else and circumvent the most sophisticated security systems. *They've stolen my snacks* and eaten them in front of me from the safety of a tree branch high above my head. That's evidence of raw, unchained evil for you, right there.

Know how many clowns have done that to me? Zero. And if a clown wants to try anything, how fast is he going to move in those oversize clown shoes? Not fast enough, no sir. He certainly won't be climbing a tree in them.

Whenever I try to convince Atticus that squirrels are most definitely involved in a shadowy plot to kill us all, though, he dismisses it and says, "I should have named you Mulder," because apparently, I've crossed a line somewhere that makes me an unhinged conspiracy theorist.

But Orlaith believes me, and Starbuck too. Starbuck is starting to learn some words, and so far he has divided the world into <Yes food!> and <No squirrel!> demonstrating that he's got a fine head on his shoulders, even if his ears are sort of batlike and his face is all smooshed in without a proper snout, like all Boston terriers.

I bring up the Looming Squirrel Peril because of what happened on the train to Portland. Atticus and I had met Starbuck in that city and adopted him after his human died, but we both wanted to go back and show Orlaith around. There were parks laid out all over it and some of them were bound to have rabbits hiding in them, and there was also that one pie bar that made some pretty fine chicken pot pies with a delicious gravy inside.

After we saved Jack the poodle and brought him back to Eugene, reuniting him with his human, Atticus thought maybe he should stop renting stuff and buy a vehicle to drive around in, since Orlaith couldn't shift planes until after she'd dropped her litter. He bought an old truck that he said was a classic, a 1954 Chevrolet. He got it for cheap since it had a lot of rust damage, but he didn't care about that. He called on Ferris, the iron elemental, to help him get rid of the rust and rebuild the steel where necessary. It was a few days' work restoring it and painting it a shiny blue, and by the time he was done and asked us where we should go, we told him we wanted to go smell all the things in Portland.

"*All* the things?" he said.

<It's a heroic quest, Atticus. At the end when we're too tired to go on, Starbuck will say, "I may not be able to smell all the things, Mr. Oberon, but I can smell you!" and then the giant eagles will swoop down out of the volcanic ash and pick us up and fly us back home, which is really the first of like twenty million endings, and we'll add forty million more in the director's cut.>

Atticus said he'd never let me watch *Lord of the Rings* again, but then he added that the truck got terrible gas mileage and he didn't want to drive it anywhere but Eugene and back, so that's why we wound up taking the train and running across the path of the most diabolical squirrel in the world. At least the ride to Eugene was great. Orlaith and I stuck our heads out the window to sample all the scents of the Willamette, and Starbuck squeezed in between us and sneezed a lot.

<Yes food!> Starbuck said, which meant he was happy. Or hungry. If I'm being honest, sometimes those things smoosh together into the same thing with us hounds.

The train station didn't smell particularly good. I'm not sure any train station, anywhere, is super-duper fragrant in the positive sense. If you want to make your nose happy, train stations are unlikely to make your top five million list. I mean, there's a lot of urine, and that's interesting, no doubt—don't get me started on fire hydrants!—but it's not what you seek out if you're in search of something pleasant. It should smell like food if it wants to impress me, but instead it smells like mothballs and cleaning products and this stuff Atticus says is an unholy body spray marketed to teenage boys.

Atticus bought two business class tickets for himself and planned to smuggle us on the train since hounds of our size just aren't allowed. The train bosses said you have to be Chihuahua class and fit under the seat to travel with your humans, but luckily Atticus didn't much care for that rule. He cast camouflage on us and told us to be quiet while boarding, and we all agreed just before we saw a squirrel on top of the train car and promptly forgot our promise. We got to woofin' and that squirrel chittered once and looked around for us, his tail swishing while the rest of him stood still.

Atticus's mental voice shouted loud in my head: *Stop that right now!* And he must have done the same to Orlaith and Starbuck, because they stopped barking too.

<But there's a squirrel, Atticus—> I began.

<No squirrel!> Starbuck added, and Orlaith started to say something too, but Atticus didn't let us get any further.

The squirrel isn't hurting anything, but your barking is hurting our chances of getting on this train without any trouble. He was looking around like all the other humans in the station, pretending he didn't know where the barking came from. *Forget about the squirrel.*

When Atticus gets like that, his voice all commanding and tense, the thing to do is back up and be patient with your explanation. It works better than bulling forward because then he just gets angrier and won't listen.

<Okay, okay. I know the squirrel isn't hurting anything right this second, Atticus, but it's only rational to assume that he is here to assassinate us.>

That's not rational at all.

<It's our duty to protect you and protect this train from whatever he's planning. We must defy the devil.>

Oberon, there's no way that squirrel can derail the train or do any other damage to it. We'll be fine. And if the squirrel tries to ride along, you know what will happen?

<What?>

He'll be blown away by the wind. There's nothing to hold on to up there. If he's dumb enough to stay on the train, physics will take care of him.

<Oh, death by physics! That sounds like justice to me,> Orlaith said.

<No squirrel!> Starbuck agreed.

<Physics is usually how people die in space, isn't it, Atticus? Unless an alien eats you or explodes out of your chest or brain weevils lay eggs in your skull or a pathogen escapes from the lab due to poor quarantine procedures—>

Right. You can enjoy imagining the many possible deaths of the squirrel once we're aboard. I need you all to be very quiet for the entire trip. Talk to me mentally all you want, but no barks or growls of any kind. Just ignore that squirrel. Leave him to physics, all right?

We agreed and got on board with no more fuss, though we saw some people point at the squirrel and say, "Aww, how cute!"

as if the squirrel didn't want them all dead. They wouldn't have said that if a clown had been staring down at them from the top of the train, would they? Nope. They would have retreated to a bunker and laid down suppressing fire before lobbing some grenades at it.

I heard Orlaith jump up into the seat next to Atticus and curl up as best as she could. I laid down on the floor and Starbuck laid down on top of me, sphinx-style, after much circling around and trying to figure out where I was. The people who sat across the aisle from us had no idea we were there. Above us, we heard the squirrel skittering around.

I'll take the camouflage off you once we're well underway and they can't throw us off the train, Atticus said. *I won't be able to maintain camouflage for very long in any case. You'll need to remain quiet the whole trip, though, especially once people know you're here.*

<Do you hear the squirrel, Atticus?>

Yes. He poses no danger, I assure you.

<Will you be able to sense when he's destroyed by physics?> Orlaith asked.

Probably not. There will be too much noise from the train moving at that point.

<Hey, why is a squirrel on the train anyway?> I said. <You don't think he's a commuter, do you? Maybe popping into Portland for the artisanal rustic nuts?>

I'm sure he doesn't even know he's on a train, much less where it's going, Atticus replied.

<Can't you do your Druid thing and find out? Rummage around in his tiny pea brain and see what he's up to?>

No, that kind of binding requires line of sight, and I can't spare the energy anyway. Settle in, now. I'm going to read you a story while we ride.

Atticus pulled out a book called *Wake of Vultures* by Lila Bowen and read to us through our mental link so other humans wouldn't think he was reading aloud to himself. But what was cool is that Atticus sent us mental pictures too, and we got to imagine what things in the story smelled like. It was a fun story, full of vampires and harpies and shape-shifters in the Old West.

Soon after the train got underway he let the camouflage drop off us and we were in plain view, but the people across the way didn't even notice us for a while, since they were busy with their computers. The closest man looked super smart; he had his head shaved like Luke Cage but wore a sharp suit instead of a hoodie. When he saw us he blinked, then his eyes slid over to Atticus, and he smirked and muttered, "Portland, man."

The lady on the far side of him was so involved in her own world she didn't even notice us until an attendant came by to check if Atticus needed a snack and startled when she saw us.

"Oh! Those are...big dogs. You're not supposed to have dogs on the train."

Atticus shot us a reminder to remain quiet and still and flashed a grin at her. "Normally, no. I'm part of a pilot program with Amtrak to evaluate the feasibility of pets on the train."

<Hey, really?>

No, I'm just making this up. "So far it's going great," he continued. "You've received no complaints about my dogs, correct?"

"Well, no, but I haven't heard about this program either."

"Oh, I'm sorry." Atticus sounded truly concerned. "They should have told you. I'm sure it was just an oversight. Here. I was told to give you this. Call that number and check up on me."

He reached into this light jacket he had on and produced a business card with stuff on it.

<Wait, you're making this up but you have a card to give her?>

Give humans a business card and they'll think you're legit, at least for a little while. It's like Doctor Who's psychic paper. I made up a business card with an Amtrak logo and a phony name and number. Chances are they won't even call.

<And if they do?>

We're going to make it to Portland regardless, and if they try to apprehend us at the station, we'll just disappear. No worries.

The attendant read the card and then said, "And who are you?"

"Ah, right, that would help, wouldn't it? I'm Connor Molloy. Here, I'll give you my card too." He produced one of the cards I'd seen before, the one that said he was an animal rights activist and dog trainer.

The attendant's eyebrows shot up when she read it. "Dog trainer, eh? Well, they're certainly well trained."

Atticus nodded. "They're very good hounds. They deserve a snack."

We all looked at Atticus when he said that and our tails thumped against the seats. Or at least, mine and Orlaith's did. Poor Starbuck just has a little stump of a tail.

The attendant laughed. "They seem to know that word."

"Yes, they're very smart. But they'll get their snack after a successful, quiet train ride."

<Aww. You could give us one in good faith as a sort of down payment.>

If you all remain silent until we're off the train, I'll find you something covered in gravy. That's better than a snack.

<A mystery meat covered in gravy? You got yourself a deal!>

The attendant turned around and asked the people across from us if we'd been any sort of bother at all. The sharp-dressed man said no, he hadn't heard a peep out of us. The lady on the other side of him said she hadn't even realized we were there until now. This satisfied the attendant and after another glance at his card, said, "Pleasant trip, Mr. Molloy."

"Thanks."

Atticus went back to reading and I guess they never checked up on his false story because no one bothered us, and you know what? That book he was reading was so good we forgot completely about the squirrel on the train!

Until we got to Portland, that is, and disembarked, and saw that same squirrel chittering at us! We weren't in camouflage now and he could see us just fine. And it was okay to bark at him because Atticus said we only had to be silent until we got off the train.

<Atticus, look!> I said while I was barking. <The squirrel made it!>

<That squirrel defies the laws of physics! Nuke it from orbit!> Orlaith said, and Starbuck added, <No squirrel!>

"Huh," Atticus said aloud, no longer bothering to keep things private in the bustle of the train station. "He must have hidden between cars."

<You didn't mention that was an option before!> I said.

"I didn't think he'd be that determined to get to Portland. I assumed he would jump off once the train started moving."

<I told you he was up to something! We must destroy him!>

"What? Oberon—"

At that moment the squirrel took off for the front of the train, running along the edge, and the chase was on. He'd run out of train eventually and he'd have to come down, and we'd be waiting to pounce. If people would get out of the way—oops! Sorry, dude! Important hound business!

So many noises and things and stuff to dodge around on top of a squirrel to keep track of—I think Atticus was shouting for us to stop but he couldn't be serious. There was a public hazard afoot! And though I shouldn't have to state the obvious, I would like the record to show that everything that happened was the squirrel's fault.

Ahead of us, we saw the squirrel leap from the roof of the train to the roof of a thingie like a veranda—it was just some posts holding up some shelter from the rain, where people would wait to board the train in between tracks—and I panicked for a moment, thinking we'd lose him forever. But then he did a spidery trick where he flipped down over the edge and leapt to a supporting post, and he scurried down it like it was a skinny tree trunk. Oh, we had him now!

He scampered across the first two tracks and slipped into the station with us on his tail. It was a terrible place to run, all slick stone floors, and sounds echoed off the surfaces. It was big and open, though, with benches like church pews in the middle, islands of wood in a sea of marble.

He dodged around a couple of corners, our nails scrambled for purchase on the tiles, and for some reason people seemed more scared of me and Orlaith and Starbuck than the squirrel. Didn't they know their enemy? We're supposed to be humans' best friends! But then the squirrel decided he didn't much like all those people clomping around either and he whipped to the right toward the baggage claim area and headed straight for this doorway marked STAIRS that a police officer was opening. Was he running for the police? It was he who'd broken all natural laws!

The police officer was startled by the squirrel zipping past him and he said, "Jesus, what the hell—" and then he added, "Christ!" when we three hounds muscled past him into the stairwell.

But halfway up there were all these humans in the way, milling around the landing. They were seriously blocking our path, and apparently unhappy that we were coming their way. One of them, a woman with long dark hair and kinda darker skin, stepped forward and shouted at us.

"Stop! You stop right now!"

I would have ignored her in the interest of public safety except that I got a whiff of her breakfast—hot sauce and eggs and some terrible coffee—and recognized who it was: Detective Gabriela Ibarra. She was all about public safety.

<Hey, whoa!> I said to the others, and put on the brakes. <We have to stop. I know this lady.>

<But the squirrel's getting away!> Orlaith said, and she was right. He was already past the humans and up the next flight. Maybe he wouldn't be able to get through the door at the top though.

<No squirrel!> Starbuck chimed in.

<It'll be okay. I think we disrupted his plans, at least.>

So we pulled up in front of Detective Ibarra and stared at her, panting, while she crossed her arms and frowned at us.

"Irish wolfhounds and a Boston terrier? Where have I seen that before? Are you here for Mr. Molloy?"

Well, not *for* him, but *because* of him, maybe? I couldn't tell her. I noticed that all the people blocking the stairwell were police. That was strange.

"I think I recognize you two, anyway," she said, pointing at me and Starbuck, "but I don't recognize this other one. My, you're gorgeous."

Orlaith preened at the praise. <Is she okay, Oberon?>

<She doesn't trust Atticus because he lies to her a lot, but yeah, I think she's all right otherwise. Not a cat person, at least.>

The detective squatted on the edge of the landing and looked at me face to face. "Are you looking for your man? Do you know what led him up here?"

I cocked my head at her. What was she talking about? As far as I knew, *we* had led him up here. Or would, anyway. I could hear him calling my name in my head and I told him where we were. I wished I could ask Detective Ibarra if she'd make sure the squirrel didn't get away upstairs, but she wasn't bound to us, so all I could do was woof at her gently.

"Well, I don't know what's going to happen to you, but I'll try to make sure you get placed with someone kind."

That made no sense at all. Come to think of it, what was the detective doing here? Weren't they supposed to be in police stations, unless they're at the scene of a…crime? Something didn't smell right. And I didn't mean the terrible coffee on her breath.

<Something's dead,> Orlaith said as soon as I thought it myself, and Starbuck quivered and whimpered. His human had died and he didn't like that smell.

Atticus came through the door behind us and said, "There you are!" and then he pulled up short when the police officer who'd come behind us put a hand on his chest. "Detective Ibarra?"

The detective rose and her face did that thing that humans do sometimes when you lick their toes unexpectedly: The eyes get real big and the mouth drops open.

"Connor Molloy? What are you doing here?"

"Chasing after my dogs. Sorry if they gave you any trouble."

The detective recovered from her surprise and squinted at him even though there wasn't any sunlight shining in her eyes. Atticus said people do that when they don't trust someone. "Let him by, Sergeant." The cop stepped aside and Atticus took a couple of steps behind us. "Do you have a twin brother?"

"Nope. Only child."

"Huh. Interesting. I don't believe you, of course. Come here but don't step on the landing."

Atticus kept coming and squeezed next to us as the detective pointed at a body on the landing with red curly hair and—great big bears!

<Atticus, he looks just like you!> He had a red mustache around his mouth in addition to the whiskers on his chin, but otherwise they looked identical.

"If you'll excuse the pun, Mr. Molloy," the detective said, "he's a dead ringer."

CHAPTER 2

BEARING UP
UNDER
PRESSURE

<I'm going to take a wild guess and say that bolt through his brain was the cause of death,> I said. It was in the middle of his forehead with a little bit of blood around it but there wasn't any on the cement—the stairs were the cold industrial kind—so the bolt didn't go all the way through. The funny thing about it was that it didn't look like it was made of wood. Unless it was painted white. Atticus commented on it.

"Is that thing in his head made of plastic?"

"Yes. We're pretty sure it's from a 3D printer but won't know for sure until we get it to the lab."

"But that's not a stabbing weapon. It looks like someone shot it into him. A blowgun wouldn't necessarily have the force to penetrate bone, so I'd say a miniature crossbow, probably also 3D printed."

"Quite possible."

"So who is he?"

"I was hoping you could tell me."

"No, I told you, I don't have any siblings or even cousins. This is just an uncanny resemblance. A really disturbing resemblance."

Hey, hounds, Atticus said to all three of us, *please start sniffing around. See if you pick up anything weird on the stairs where the shot came from, a scent that doesn't belong to any of the police officers here.*

<There are lots of smells,> Orlaith replied. <It's a public place.>

I know. But this stairwell is probably not used by everyone. Just see if anything stands out.

"So he had no ID?" he asked the detective.

"No, and no keys, no phone, no receipts in his pockets to help us reconstruct his last hours. Somebody rolled him good."

"Do you know if he was killed here or somewhere else, and dragged here?"

"I know I should be asking *you* some questions. Why are you in Portland right now?"

"The dogs like to smell stuff and Portland has lots of stuff."

"This isn't a time to be flippant," Ibarra said, her voice taking on a tone of irritation, but I didn't understand why. Atticus was telling her the truth! "Has it occurred to you that, considering your resemblance, maybe *you* were the target here and this guy got killed by mistake?"

"Yeah, it has." It hadn't occurred to me, but now I was worried. Atticus had lots of enemies. And it was a chilly morning, so the dead guy had bundled up with coat and gloves, covering up the arm and hand that would have Druidic tattoos on it. Easy to mistake their identities.

"So why are you in Portland? Are you up to something that might make you a target?"

"Not at the moment; I'm honestly here to have fun with the hounds, and we just got here on the train from Eugene. But my past as an animal rights activist may have angered some people."

<Ha! That's one way of putting it,> I said to Atticus.

"Can you list them for me?" the detective asked.

<I can! The Norse pantheon, the Egyptian pantheon, the Roman goddess of the hunt, most of the Fae, and all the vampires...>

"Sure, but I can already tell you they're not the kind of people who would think of using 3D printed weapons. They're ranchers and have plenty of old-school weapons, plus those little flags with a coiled snake on it, you know, the kind of people who complain about 'the gubbermint' and like to quote that Jefferson line about watering the tree of liberty with the blood of tyrants."

Now Atticus was just making stuff up, I could tell. But I didn't hear the detective's reply because Orlaith called me and

Starbuck from a few steps down. <Hey, you guys, come smell this and see if you're picking up what I am. It's weird.>

Orlaith was snuffling around the handrail on the fourth step, and our nails clicked on the cement as we went to join her. We snuffled around where her nose was and sure enough, mixed in with all the random human scents was something else. Not very old, either.

<Am I right?> Orlaith asked. <You smell it, too?>

<Yes food!> Starbuck replied.

<Yeah, I got it. That's not normal. That shouldn't be here. We gotta tell Atticus!> I called to him and he asked us to wait one moment while he disengaged with the detective. They traded business cards, Atticus assuring her that the phone number on there was current and he'd be in town all day, and then he came over to join us.

What is it, buddy? he asked me privately.

<You know how werewolves always smell mostly human but with a little bit of wolf mixed in—what's that fancy word for "just a little bit" you taught me, has something to do with soup?>

Soupçon.

<Right. Well, right here on this handrail, we're getting a human female with a soupçon of great big bear.>

Atticus frowned. *You're absolutely positive about that? You're sure it's a bear?*

<Only one thing that smells like bear, and that's bear. On a handrail in a train station.>

And you're sure it's a female?

<Yeah. There's a hint of blood. She's doing that thing humans do. Medication.>

I think you mean menstruation.

<Right, that's what I said.>

Atticus turned to look over his shoulder at the police, and they all had their backs to us, considering the body. He pulled leashes out of his jacket.

Okay, you three. I think you may have found a genuine clue. I want you to follow that scent out of here, taking your time. We're going at a walking pace until we're out of the station so that no one gets alarmed. We can speed up after that if you're confident of the trail.

<Hey, are we fighting crime again?>

Yes, if you don't mind. I'd like to know who murdered my doppelgänger.

<Yes! I was hoping we'd get to solve another murder sometime!>

<What's a doppelgänger?> Orlaith asked.

It's a German word coined by Johann Paul Richter. Doppel means "double" and gänger *means "goer," and originally it was meant to refer to a spirit self that's invisible but identical to you. Now it can mean anyone who appears to be a copy of you, like a clone, or sometimes it refers to an evil twin.*

<So that means there's a spirit Orlaith that looks like me? Does she have spirit puppies in her belly and eat spirit sausages when she's hungry?>

We can only hope. If so, she's invisible.

<Whoa, Atticus, whoa!> I said. <This is blowing my mind. You mean we're walking in a world filled with invisible sausages right now?>

Maybe. It's nice to think so, isn't it?

He clipped leashes to our collars and we slinked past the police sergeant at the bottom of the stairs and set off on the trail, which doubled back on itself and then forked. <One goes to the platform and one out of the station,> I said.

Let's follow the one out of the station, Atticus replied, and then we were out in Portland, land of many smells, but following the Great Big Bear That Did Not Belong.

We had ourselves a good long trek after that, following the scent to the West Hills and Washington Park, breaking into a pretty decent jog. We were catching up, in fact; the scent got fresher and stronger as we went.

Inside Washington Park there are smaller parks laid out. There's an International Rose Test Garden, though I'm not sure how well roses can be expected to score on a test. There's an arboretum too, which I've never been to before but which sounds magical, because it's full of strange and wonderful trees to pee on! But there's also a Japanese Garden, five and a half acres of lush vegetation and stone paths around ponds, bridges and waterfalls and stone lanterns, all of it contributing to a sense of serenity. The bear scent led us there. It led us straight to a stone bench, in fact, overlooking a calm expanse of water. It was still pretty chilly out so the park wasn't all green and humming with insects like it would be in summer, but it still had a wintry beauty to it.

There was a large person sitting on the bench wearing a big poufy black coat, and with their head down it seemed from a distance like we were looking at a giant gumdrop. I couldn't tell if the person was actually large or if their poufy coat was providing all the bulk. Atticus stopped us well before I could figure it out, though, and called a name. Did he already know who we were tracking?

"Suluk?" he said, and the person turned around. There wasn't a trace of whiskers so I was going to guess it was a woman, especially since we had been tracking a woman. She blinked dark eyes in a broad face a few times. "Suluk Black? Is that you?"

"Are you a ghost, come to haunt me?" she said.

"I'm your old friend, Siodhachan. That man in the train station wasn't me."

She blinked a couple of times more and then she stood, turned fully in our direction, and her face broke into a hopeful grin. "You're still alive?"

"For the moment. You're not out to get me, are you?"

Her smile disappeared and she shook her head violently. "No, no! That wasn't me!"

"Okay to come closer?"

"Yeah, sure. Your dogs won't come after me, will they?"

"Nah. Give me a second to make sure, though." And then Atticus's voice was in our heads. *Listen, Suluk Black is the daughter of Kodiak Black. She's a bear shifter, and that's what you were smelling. Which means, yes, she is at times a great big bear and not your favorite animal in the world. But she is a good friend of mine and will be a good friend of yours. So not a single growl in her direction, hear me? Be very polite.*

<Okay,> I said, and Orlaith and Starbuck agreed too. <Is Suluk her real name?>

No. It's a name she chose and held onto, like I chose Atticus. I don't know her real name.

We trotted over there and I only sniffed at the air a couple of times to confirm that this was the person we had been following.

"It's been a long time," Atticus said. "I had no idea you were here."

"Oh yes, I've been here fifteen years now. Great farmers' markets in the summer."

"Yeah, right? Listen, I'm very sorry about Kodiak."

"Thank you. I heard his killer paid for it, though. The circle is closed."

"Are you well?"

Suluk sighed before answering. "I'm shaken by what I saw, but relieved now that I know it wasn't you."

"Would you mind telling me what happened?"

"Yes. But I don't want to talk to the police about it."

"I won't share anything with them. But it's best that you leave town anyway, maybe spend some time as a bear. They might pull your image off of security cameras."

"That sounds like a good idea. Sit with me?"

They sat on the stone bench, staring at the pond instead of each other, so we hounds all sat on the grass nearby, staring at the same pond. There weren't any fish jumping in it, or even kissing the surface with their little fish lips and making ripples. But I knew they were there, invisible, just like all those sausages Atticus was talking about.

<Just think, Orlaith,> I said. <We are surrounded by unseen deliciousness with every step we take. It is at once tragic and hopeful. The kind of thing that sells millions of copies. I should write an inspirational book called *All the Food We Cannot See*.>

<Oh, that would be great!>

<Yes food!> Starbuck said. We didn't discuss it anymore though, because Atticus started asking questions and we wanted to know what happened in the train station.

"Walk me through it," he said to Suluk, and her voice changed a little bit, a storyteller's cadence.

"I was in the station to see someone off to Eugene—the 6 a.m. Cascades line, same as yours, just going the other way. After the train rolled out I saw a flash of red hair across the platform and it reminded me of you. And then when I took a better look, I thought it *was* you. But he was moving away from me and there were too many people in between us to call out. So I hurried after, trying to keep him in sight, and he ducked into that stairwell—I don't even know where it goes. But it felt like a place we could talk, at least, so I shouted after him to wait up. I caught up to him on the landing and I swear I thought he was you. I smiled at him and asked if he remembered me, but the door opened behind us and his eyes kind of slid off me and then widened at something over my shoulder. I turned to see what it was—rotated to my right so my back was against the wall—and gave the killer a clean shot. I can't tell you much about whoever it was. Bulky winter jacket like mine, gloves, a balaclava and sunglasses covering the face. Can't even tell you if it was a man or woman. They moved fast, though. They had a miniature crossbow already aimed, and they shot that man right in front of me. Once your twin hit the ground they were out of there."

"They didn't say anything first, just shot and ran?"

"Yeah. It wasn't random mugging or anything. It was a targeted hit."

"And they took off immediately? They didn't go through his pockets?"

"No, that was me."

"What?"

Suluk stuck a gloved hand into her jacket and pulled out a wallet. "I knew if it was you that you'd have an alias, but I didn't know what you were calling yourself these days. I thought maybe I could do something, you know? Because whoever's killing Druids sure isn't on my side." She handed over the wallet and Atticus just held it, considering.

"Okay, I need to amend what I said earlier: The police are *definitely* going to be looking for you. I mean, they'll be looking for the man or woman with the balaclava too, but they're going to see you coming out of that stairway after him and know you witnessed the murder."

"I kept my hood up and my head down."

"But not the entire time you were in the station, right? They'll scroll backward and find you on the platform saying farewell to your friend. They might even be able to attach a name to your face, and your friend too—you should give them a heads-up that the police might drop by."

She sighed a grumbly sigh. "Definitely time to bear up, then."

"Indeed." Atticus gave her one of his cards. "I'm Connor Molloy these days, and I've got a place on the McKenzie River."

"So you're close! That's a nice area."

"You're welcome to visit anytime. Maybe we can work up a new identity for you."

"I might just do that. I'll call first, though. Wouldn't want to upset the hounds." She turned and spoke to us, correctly assuming we'd understand her. "Thank you for tolerating my presence. You're fantastic hounds."

All three of us stared back at her, ears up, utterly stunned until I could muster a mental whisper to Orlaith. <Did I...did we just get a compliment from a bear?>

<What do we do?> Orlaith said. <Should we be mad or happy or what?>

<I think we're still supposed to be polite. But I don't think this has ever happened before. I didn't know it was possible! You know what this means, Orlaith? We're surrounded by invisible kindness too, always waiting to surprise us! But it's a happy surprise! I should probably devote a chapter to it in my book.>

<Yes, I'd like to read that!>

Suluk gave Atticus a set of keys also taken from the doppel-gänger's pockets and he asked if there was a phone. She shrugged, said she didn't find one, and then they hugged and said human farewell things. She waved at us and we gave her a good-bye woof as she walked away into the park. I thought we would be leaving then too but Atticus sat back down on the bench.

"Now," he said, opening the wallet to look at the ID. "Let's find out who my look-alike was."

CHAPTER 3

THE GUY
WHO HID
THE SAUSAGE

Atticus snorted at the driver's license. "Hudson Keane? Who names their Irish kid *Hudson?*"

<Somebody who's wrong a lot?> I guessed.

"I'd say so. Hmm. Twenty-two years old. Address here in Portland, not too far. But we probably shouldn't go there without Detective Ibarra. If I go there and don't share this info she won't be cool with that and will never share anything with us."

<Are you trying to establish that give-and-take relationship you call *Squid Pro Go?*>

"What? You mean *quid pro quo?*"

<Well, I don't know. Maybe? But I hope not. I was rather hoping to meet a squid pro someday.>

"What the heck is a squid pro?"

<I don't know, that's why I wanted to meet one!>

"Add it to the bucket list, I guess." He took off our leashes and said we could roam as long as we kept him in sight and didn't harass anyone. "We're heading back down to the park entrance."

Orlaith and Starbuck kind of wandered off a wee bit to smell and pee on trees, but I stayed right by the side of my Druid as he pulled out his phone and Detective Ibarra's card.

"Don't you want to go smell some stuff, Oberon? It's why we came up here."

<Well, yeah, but that squirrel changed things, didn't he? We're on a case now, Atticus. And someone may be after you. That means I'm on guard duty until it's over.>

"Okay. I appreciate it, buddy. You know what? I like this spot. Think I'll bind a tree to Tír na nÓg here so we can come back easily. Then I'll call the detective and put her on speaker so you can hear."

I could hear the detective's impatience when she answered his call, but much of the richness of her voice was gone, strained and tinny sounding through the phone. What happens to human voices when they travel through phones? Is there some kind of monster living in the in-between spaces, feeding on their expression and tone? Something that lives on timbre? I might need to include a chapter in my book about unheard sound and what our ears so often miss.

"Yes, Detective," Atticus said. "I think I may have something to help you out. My hounds picked up a scent at the scene and we followed it all the way to Washington Park. I do believe I've found the victim's wallet."

"You mean the man who looks exactly like you?" she said.

"Yes, that's the one. Would you mind meeting me at the park entrance and we'll go to the victim's house together?"

"No, you'll just give me the wallet."

"I think I deserve some courtesy here, Detective Ibarra, for once again, I am doing a good portion of your investigative work for you in the pursuit of a murderer. Can you consider me a consultant, at least, if not an equal? I'm only trying to be helpful."

"What would be helpful is you turning over what you've found so I can do my job."

"I'll be happy to turn it over as long as you give me a ride to his house. I have an interest in finding this murderer and clearly, I can help you. Or do you know the victim's name and place of residence already?"

"God damn it, Molloy, you know I don't. What's his name?"

"Come pick me and my hounds up at the entrance to Washington Park and I'll tell you. Oh, and we found his keys too."

"Seriously? What about a cell phone?"

"Sadly not. Just the wallet and keys. But surely that will provide you more leads than what you have now? Come on, Detective. We're on the same side. Let's work together on this."

Detective Ibarra muttered something unintelligible and then arranged a pickup spot with Atticus. I chuffed in the chilly air, victorious. Druids rock.

Some time later—hours or minutes or months, I don't know—we piled into Detective Ibarra's automobile, the engineers of which never anticipated two wolfhounds jumping into the back seat. "Jesus," she kept saying, as if saying his name would make him appear and magically give us more room in her tiny car. "Do they shed a lot?"

Oh, that was a low blow, if I may use the parlance of human gladiator sports. She makes it sound like humans would never vacuum their cars if it weren't for hounds. Humans shed too, you know!

Atticus distracted her with the wallet of Hudson Keane, and we hounds were soon distracted by the many, many discarded taco wrappers behind the front seats, the legacy of stakeouts, perhaps, or just never enough time to enjoy her lunch at an actual table. Thin wax paper coated in thick layers of grease: They were the ultimate tease. I could fault the detective on her prejudice against hounds, but I could not fault her customary choice of carne asada topped with fresh cilantro. Even long dead and gone, those tacos still smelled great. They were ghost tacos, taunting us with our tardiness. Oh, ghost tacos! Why can't I quit you?

<Ask her to take us to lunch, Atticus,> I said, not even paying attention to their conversation except that they were talking about the stairwell, <and we will climb the stairway to heaven.>

He ignored me, though, because the detective switched to quizzing him for details about the wallet and keys, and their conversation eventually penetrated my greasy taco dreams. How did he find them? Where did he find them? Did he see anyone near them? Atticus was very careful to leave Suluk out of it and pretend that we led him to the wallet and keys, discarded in the park—which I suppose was partially true. We did lead him to the park.

When we got to the apartment complex of Hudson Keane, Atticus put leashes on us again at the insistence of the detective. Apparently, her opinion of hounds was that we just run around contaminating crime scenes and pee everywhere we can, but that's not true. We pee wherever we *want to,* and there's a big difference.

The apartment was on the second floor. The detective called into her station or precinct or whatever it's called to inform them that she was entering the home of the victim with his keys.

Except that we didn't need to. The door was open a little bit, the lock smashed or hacked to pieces right out of the frame. When Detective Ibarra saw that, she asked us to stay back and she pulled a gun out of a shoulder holster underneath her jacket. Then she called her base again saying she needed a team out here for backup because the victim's residence had been broken into.

"I think we're getting closer to discovering a motive here," the detective said. "Don't enter until I say it's clear."

I guess she wasn't going to wait for that backup. She kicked the door open and went in low, gun pointed in front of her.

Atticus took a peek around the door jamb after a few seconds.

The place is trashed. Huh. It's starting to look like Hudson's murder wasn't a case of mistaken identity. He really was the target. What kind of naughty shit do you think he was into?

<Lizards,> I said.

I beg your pardon?

<He's got a terrarium in there and something cold-blooded lives inside it. I can smell it from here. Snaky-lizardy-reptile smell.>

Interesting. Hey, before we go in, all three of you sniff around the door jamb here and the threshold. Do you smell any scents that you also smelled in the train station—besides Hudson, I mean? Because if you find a match that might be our killer.

We applied our snoots to the scenario, snuffling around the edge of the doorway. I didn't catch anything and neither did Orlaith, but Starbuck growled at something. He recognized a scent from the train station and started pulling on his leash toward the stairs.

Found something, Starbuck? Go ahead, lead the way, but take it slow. We'll stay on the leash for now.

We followed Starbuck's sniffer downstairs and to the parking lot, where he turned sharply away from the detective's car. The trail led along a decorative plant bed near the building, almost right in it. Whoever it was had tried to hug the building and purposely didn't walk in the middle of the sidewalk.

Starbuck led us to the parking spot nearest the street, which had some kind of generic four-door sedan parked in it. I thought it would have more room in the back for wolfhounds, but not much. Starbuck led us all around the car and snorted in frustration.

<No squirrel!> he said, sitting down and laying his ears back flat against his head, sorry to give us bad news. The trail ended there.

It's okay, Starbuck, you did great! I take it this is not the killer's car but he or she was parked here earlier. Atticus walked to the back of the sedan and craned his head around at the buildings, searching for something in the complex. *Aha! See there?* He pointed at the office entrance but I had no idea what he wanted me to see.

<What is it?>

Mounted on that light pole about twice my height. Surveillance camera pointed at the parking lot. We'll get the detective to pull the footage. Oh, shit!

<What?>

We just left her and didn't say where we were going! I don't even know if the apartment was clear! Gods below, I'll never make a good cop! Come on, let's go back!

Atticus erupted into what was a long-legged stride for him but we kept up easily. As we climbed the stairs to Keane's apartment he shouted, "Detective Ibarra? Detective!"

He sighed with relief when she called back, even though she didn't sound happy to hear from him. "Yeah, I'm here. All clear. Where the hell did you go?" She had her arms crossed at the front door and was doing a human scowly-face thing. Atticus was in trouble.

Atticus shoved his hands into his pockets and broke eye contact, hunching his shoulders together, and spoke with far less confidence than he usually did. He said this was "being sheepish," but sheep don't have any pockets so I don't know what's up with that expression.

"Well, my hounds recognized a smell from the stairwell of the train station and we followed it out to the parking lot.

There's a surveillance camera there so you can probably check the tape and get the killer's license plate and maybe even a screen cap of his face."

"What?" The detective raised one hand and waggled a finger at him. "No no no no no. See, this is why we don't have consultants. There are so many things wrong with what you just did and said that I don't know where to begin."

"Okay, how about science?"

"What science?"

"The science of olfaction. Every human has a scent as unique as their fingerprints. Dogs can detect that and use it to track people. What they picked up here at the outside of the door was the same scent of someone who was in that stairwell at the train station—and I don't mean Hudson Keane."

"How in the world do you know that? Did they tell you that?"

"No, they're trained."

Heh heh! I love it when Atticus lies to other humans about talking to us. They always buy it.

"But they're not bloodhounds," the detective objected.

"Almost all dogs are capable of detecting those scents. Bloodhounds are famously good at it but the noses on my hounds are perfectly up to this. And you can train for exclusion as well as inclusion. What you see in films are people holding up a piece of clothing and telling their hounds to go find it— that's fine. But you can also train them to look for what doesn't fit that same scent profile. Find something new and follow that. That's what we did here. Starbuck—the Boston terrier—made the match. And it's fine if you don't believe me."

"I don't. You know why? Because even if you can train dogs to do that—I'm not sure it's possible—you've only had that dog for what, a couple of weeks at most?"

"He's already a trained champion and I'm very good at my job. I'm very sorry if I'm interfering with yours but I'm trying to be helpful. My hounds got us this far, at least. Checking that tape can't hurt, right? You probably would have done it anyway."

"Oh, absolutely, I would have. Because that's the sort of thing you use to build a case on, not some hipster's claim that his dog found something."

Atticus grinned back at her, not bothered at all. "Can this hipster's dogs take a sniff around before your backup arrives and tromps through there?"

"And just add dog hair to the crime scene? Uh-uh."

<Wow, she really has a thing about shedding, Atticus. She must be projecting. I bet her drain is totally clogged with hair.>

"Well, how about me? Can I take a quick peek around if I don't touch anything?"

The detective's eyes dropped down to us.

"Oh, don't worry about them. They'll stay here." *Please stay here,* Atticus added mentally, and then he squeezed past the detective before she could think of an objection. She kept watching us to see what we would do, and I thought it was weird but then I realized what she was doing: She was waiting for us to misbehave so she could use us to mess with Atticus. Sorry, Detective.

<Hey Atticus, could you investigate the refrigerator first?> I asked, looping in Orlaith and Starbuck on the joke.

<Yes food!> the Boston said.

<Yeah, I remember someone promising us something covered in gravy for being quiet on the train,> Orlaith added.

Oh, crap. I'm sorry. I don't normally forget. Things have been a little intense since we got here.

Atticus tore off a paper towel hanging from a roll mounted underneath the cabinet and the noise drew the detective's attention.

"Hey, you said you wouldn't touch anything!" she said.

"I'm just checking the fridge and not leaving any prints."

"Why?"

"Making sure there aren't any human body parts in there. And my dogs are hungry." I heard the shuffle of glass containers in the door as he opened it and I imagined what they might be. Jars of mayonnaise, probably, or pickles. Hopefully no mustard. I didn't hear anything else for a few moments so I assumed he was taking it all in, until he said, "Looks like Mr. Keane was a vegetarian."

I did my best impression of a frustrated Vizzini in *The Princess Bride*. <Gah!>

<That means there's nothing to eat!> Orlaith said. Starbuck just whimpered.

I heard Atticus open drawers and mutter as he inspected them. "Blocks of tofu, soy cheese...that's not going to work. Aha! What's this way back here?" The detective left the doorway and stopped blocking our view, so I could see him holding up a plastic baggie with something promising inside. "I do believe that this is a summer sausage, hidden from his sight and long forgotten! He must have had it for some meat-eating friends or something and never finished it. Okay if I give this to the dogs? And before you say no, Detective, remember that the only reason we're here is because of them."

She sighed, took a quick look at it, and gave in. "All right. I guess he won't be eating it. But nothing else. I need to see if I can find any electronics or his phone. The fact we haven't found any so far worries me."

"Thanks."

The detective disappeared down a hallway or something and we didn't really care what she was up to because Atticus was heading our way with sausage and that was vitally important. Orlaith and I were basically sweeping the front stoop with our tails and Starbuck, sitting between us, quivered all over with excitement.

Atticus squatted down on his haunches in front of us and smiled. "This will take the edge off until I can get you something with gravy on it, eh?" He opened the bag and a heavenly scent wafted forth. Yeah, we all drooled. But when Atticus pulled it out of the bag, a big stout cylinder of cured beef with a delightful pattern of marbled fat showing on the end that had been cut, we all realized at the same time that he didn't have any easy way to divide it up for us.

"Oh, I didn't bring a knife. That was stupid. Sorry. Hang on a second."

Orlaith asked for clarification when Atticus didn't move but just kept staring at the end of the sausage. <Uh, how long is a second, again?>

<A basically useless unit of measurement because humans use it to mean anything,> I said. <And he wonders why I have trouble telling time.>

"Wait up. This doesn't look right," Atticus said, keeping his voice low. "There's a fissure here. Or something." He put his finger and thumb to the center of the sausage and with just a little bit of effort pulled out a neat little chunklet of it, leaving a rectangular hole in it that was much deeper than the small chunk he'd pulled out.

<Auggh! He hollowed out the center of the sausage? What kind of monster would do such a thing? I tell ya, Atticus, these vegetarians have to be stopped!>

"It's hollowed out because he put something in there," Atticus nearly whispered, and tossed the small chunk at Starbuck, who snatched it out of the air and said, <Yes food!>

Atticus upended the sausage over his hand and shook it up and down. A slim black rectangle of plastic fell out of the sausage into his palm, and he didn't look at it long before standing up and pushing it into his pocket.

"Stay here, please. I'm going to go cut this up for you. Thanks for being patient."

<Wait, Atticus, what just happened? What was that thing?>

Atticus switched to his mental voice to make sure the detective didn't hear him.

I'm not sure precisely what it is yet, but there's a good chance it's what got Hudson Keane killed. No tech in the house and no phone, but we have a flash drive hidden in a sausage which was itself hidden in the back of a vegetarian's refrigerator. And very carefully, too. Neither I nor the detective saw that little cut at first glance. So whatever's on this flash drive was worth the trouble in Hudson's mind.

Atticus rummaged around the kitchen using a paper towel to touch everything so he wouldn't leave fingerprints. He found a cutting board and a knife, wrapped the towel around the handle, and began chopping.

<So what you're doing right now, besides chopping up sausage, is destroying evidence?>

Yep.

<This is probably not a *squid pro go* thing you're doing.>

Nope.

<You could get in lots of trouble if the detective found out.>

Yep.

<So why are you doing it?>

Because you're hungry. And because at this point I think our unorthodox, extra-legal methods are working much faster than conventional law enforcement. When the detective finally pulls that footage of the parking lot I'm sure she'll see the same person covered up head-to-toe with no distinguishing features and any license plate they get will turn out to be stolen. And I bet the person will disappear from the shot too after a short while; I'm sure that's why they were hugging the building walls coming in. They knew where the cameras were ahead of time. They made and used an untraceable weapon that can easily be melted down to goo. They hit him in public and ran, as professional a hit as you could imagine, except for Suluk's presence. But just think: If Suluk hadn't thought Keane looked like me and gone after him, they would have caught him all alone in that stairwell, no witnesses. So as Suluk said, this wasn't a crime of passion or a case of being in the wrong place at the wrong time. It was a well-planned assassination, and that means that there's a big

---

pile of money behind all this. And you know what that means for law enforcement?

It took me a moment, but then I got it. <They're going to run into a lot of lawyers at some point.>

Exactly. Delays and obstacles while the bad guys get away. But we're going to skirt around all of that. We're already far closer behind them than they thought anyone would be.

Atticus put down the knife and brought over the cutting board, clutching it with a paper towel. He quickly threw chunks of sausage at our mouths in turn and we caught them all, and it was all gone in about a decade or whatever.

<Yum. That was some delicious evidence,> Orlaith said, and Starbuck and I agreed. <But I'm still hungry. Are we going to get something with gravy too?>

Heck yes. Let me say goodbye to the detective and we'll go like squid pros.

Atticus no sooner said that than the detective shouted from somewhere in the apartment. "Ahh! Son of a—!"

My Druid dropped the cutting board and darted into the apartment, calling "Detective?"

"It's all right," I heard her reply. "I was just startled. That's a damn big lizard."

"Hmm. Oh, indeed. That's one impressive iguana. Out of his terrarium." Privately Atticus shot a thought to me: *You called it, buddy. Lizard in the house.*

<Mmm, iguana! Chicken of the trees!> I may have been licking the cutting board at that precise instant but I am very talented and can ingest sausage residue and think about chicken at the same time.

"Yeah," Detective Ibarra said. "Look at how it's all messed up, the rocks and sand and shit all over. They were looking for something in there."

Atticus knew exactly what they were looking for because it was already in his pocket. But he said, "Huh. That's strange. Well, look, Detective, I've fed my hounds and don't wish to intrude any more than I already have. But I would really love to help some more if I can. Will you call me, please, and let me know what you find out about Hudson Keane? I'll be returning to Eugene tonight but I'm also flexible. I'm at your service if you need me."

"Yeah, all right. Thanks, Molloy. I'll call you when we know something."

We reached the bottom of the stairs as Detective Ibarra's backup arrived in the parking lot. We three hounds walked out of the complex with our Druid walking us on leashes, but they weren't holding us back, no sir. We were way ahead of the police and headed for justice—and gravy, of course. If you think about it, they're almost the same thing.

CHAPTER 4

THE CRYPTO KEEPER

Atticus led us to Random Order Pie Bar so we three hounds could enjoy the rich gravy of their pot pies, for he had made a Solemn Gravy Promise earlier and needed to keep it. While we were eating, he made a phone call and we listened in to his side of it.

"Hi, Earnest. Connor Molloy here. Say, since you're a computer wiz of sorts, I wondered if you might have a standalone machine handy on which to try suspicious flash drives, check for viruses, things like that, without being on the net. You do? Fantastic. Might I trouble to you inspect something? I promise to pay you for your time, and if it turns out to be something terrible that destroys your machine, I promise to replace it." He paused to let Earnest reply, then said, "Absolutely. I'll drop by this evening if you wouldn't mind sharing your address. And what do you like to drink? I'll bring some of that too, then. Thanks."

<Was that Earnest Goggins-Smythe, the human of Jack the poodle and Algy the boxer?> We had met them recently because Jack had been kidnapped and we rescued him.

"It was. We'll see them when we get back to Eugene."

He made another call to an actual private investigator in town and we swung by there to pay them some money. He wanted a background check on Hunter Keane and some family history as soon as possible. After that there was nothing for us to do until we saw Earnest that night, and we were finally able to enjoy Portland's parks and smell things.

That did mean, however, that by the time we returned to the train station for the afternoon ride home, we were pretty dang tired, giving the train only a cursory inspection for squirrels before boarding and curling up for a nap. We never did find out if the squirrel got out of the stairwell or not.

When we arrived in Eugene Atticus told us that he got a couple of calls while we slept. He filled us in on the way out to the truck and on the way to Earnest's house.

"The reason Hudson Keane looked so much like me is because he was a descendant of mine, albeit many generations removed. I'd been trying to hide from Aenghus Óg in New York in the late nineteenth century, and my relationship with a woman back then resulted in his birth more than a century later."

<Oh, suffering cats, Atticus, I'm sorry.>

"Yes, it's very sad. Hudson looked to have a bright future and seemed to have inherited my paranoia along with his features."

<What do you mean?>

"The reason the police never found a phone was because he didn't own one, so far as they know. If he had one, he used burners only, like me. And his digital footprint is absurdly small. He has a bank card but only uses it to buy coffee at different shops around the city—he was purposely all over the place. All his other financial transactions are deposits and withdrawals of cash with no clear indication of where it's coming from. He's unemployed, so far as the world is concerned, yet he clearly has an off-the-books income from somewhere. The best guess we can make right now was he was doing some kind of super-secret science."

<What kind? Not Weird Science?>

"Hudson graduated from M.I.T. last year with a chemical engineering degree. Which means he graduated from both high school and college early. Big brain, in other words, and in the employ of someone who wants no clear records of his employment. At this point I'm just hoping it's not narcotics."

<Does he have a secret lab somewhere behind a bookcase and you have to pull out a volume of Paracelsus to make it open? Wait! Atticus, what if he's one of the guys working on the elusive Triple Nonfat Double Bacon Five-Cheese Mocha, as foretold in the prophecy?>

"Gods below, I'd forgotten about that. You never did tell me where you heard such a thing, but regardless, I think we'll find the answer on that flash drive."

Earnest Goggins-Smythe was a very nice guy with an unfortunate foot odor problem and a habit of wearing T-shirts he bought at Comic Cons. This time he wore one from the movie *Tucker and Dale vs. Evil*. Atticus said he was a British expatriate, which may or may not be the same as an ex-patriot; he said such things were complicated.

Earnest worked from home as some kind of I.T. professional and showed dogs on the side, so I doubted he owned any other clothes except for one suit he wore on the show circuit. He practically ignored Atticus and just paid attention to me, Orlaith, and Starbuck when we arrived, asking only if we could have snacks, which Atticus agreed to. Atticus watched him pet us and make silly noises for a few years while he looked around.

We were in a sort of living room that Earnest had tricked out to be an extra-large office. He had one of those extra-long wooden tables you find in libraries with reading lamps at either end, a kind of deluxe office chair at his work station, but a couple of wooden dining room chairs down at the other side. His work area had three different monitors and two keyboards. He had some code on one that looked like something from *The Matrix*, a video game paused on another, and the sci-fi movie *Arrival* playing at low volume on a third, because I recognized the heptapod noises.

He told Atticus in his British accent, "Laptop's on the end, ready to go. It doesn't have much on it in the way of apps besides antivirus software. Run them all on your flash drive and then we'll see what you have on my station."

Atticus thanked him and I shot him a mental request. <Hey, tell me what you're doing and seeing while I'm getting bathed in adorations over here?>

Sure thing, buddy.

Earnest asked him if it would be okay to take us out back to play with Jack and Algy, and Atticus said that would be fine. In less time than it takes for a badger to get angry we were outside smelling asses and having a great time.

I was already in a friendly, chewy boxing match with Algy when Atticus told me what was on the flash drive.

There are three encrypted files on here. And I have three decrypt keys provided by Detective Ibarra.

<She gave you decrypt keys for the evidence you stole?>

She had no idea they were decrypt keys. They were just three strings of 64 digits each they found in his apartment taped to the inside of his closet wall and she thought it was a code instead of the key to something else. She thought it would be harmless to give them to me, though I did have to ask to see them.

<Ha ha! You, harmless?>

Running virus scans on here now. I'm sure it'll be fine but best to be sure. How are you doing?

<Orlaith just tagged in against Algy and she took him down. He couldn't believe it and he's all rambunctious now. You know, *rambunctious* is one of those words that's as fun to say as it is to *be*.>

I got rambunctious after that and lost some time playing around. But eventually Atticus came outside and told Earnest the flash drive was all clear and he'd like to take a look at the files on the sweet custom setup.

Earnest said we should just keep playing while they went inside and I reminded Atticus to keep the play-by-play going.

All right. First file decrypting...huh. It's a Word file with the title Stable Solar. Opening now, doing a bit of speed reading...holy shit.

<What is it?>

Well, uh, it would seem my descendant was a genius who had solved the world's energy problems. Which would basically pit him against everybody currently producing energy. No wonder he was paranoid.

<But solar, though? I thought that was already a thing.>

It is a thing, but the only reasons solar hasn't already wiped out gas and coal and the rest of it entirely is because it's inefficient, and to keep the lights on at night you'd need much better battery storage than we currently have. He's claiming here to have solved both problems. He's increased the solar efficiency of Perovskite cells to forty-nine percent—that's really high, you could make solar practical in the upper latitudes with that—and he says he's figured out a way to stabilize the rapid degradation of Perovskite surfaces in humid environments. And he also has some kind of new rechargeable battery that will store the excess electricity for nighttime usage. Well, now we know why he was killed.

<Is there any proof this is real?>

I'm assuming the other two files are schematics for the cells and the battery, but we'll see. Point is, even the threat of this being real would get him killed, and he knew it. So he was operating as anonymously as possible.

<So that's why his place was trashed. They were looking for this. Which means they'll be looking for you.>

Nobody knows I have it except you, and you won't tell anyone. And they might not be aware it exists. They probably have his computer and think that's sufficient. If they're looking for anyone, it's for the person listed on the paper here with him: Ignacio Medina, PhD. He was the electrical engineer part of the team. I need to call the detective. But let me confirm what these other files are first...

<Wait, Atticus, are you going to tell her you stole that from the scene? She'll put you in jail!>

No, I'm just going to get her to look for Dr. Medina. Hmm. Yep, these other files are schematics for world-changing tech. That tells us why Hudson was killed. We just don't know who did it.

<I want to hear the phone call with the detective! Let me in!>

Sure. Let's go, I've got what I need here.

I gave Algy and Jack friendly nips on the ear as a good-bye and Atticus retrieved us from the backyard. He said thank you and goodbye to Earnest without biting his ear and dialed Detective Ibarra from the cab of the truck.

"You might already know this, Detective, but Hudson Keane was working closely with a Dr. Ignacio Medina. Might be a good idea to track him down."

"No, I hadn't heard this. How did you find out?"

"A private investigator."

"Okay, who?"

"I'd like to keep that private."

The detective sighed. "You really can't. Look, Molloy, on the one hand I appreciate your help. Sincerely. But on the other, your methods are the kind of thing that defense lawyers love to use to create a reasonable doubt. They will either take apart your testimony or get your evidence tossed out because we can't account for how it was gained, you see? So if you want to continue to help we need you to be more forthcoming, or I need you to get your P.I. license or become a registered informant with the department. I'm already getting a headache trying to figure out how to report you finding the missing wallet and keys."

"Okay, I confess. This isn't really Connor Molloy but some-one else using his phone to give you an anonymous tip on the Keane murder. Ignacio Medina worked with the victim. He may know something."

"Damn it—" Ibarra said before Atticus ended the call with his thumb.

<You keep making her mad, Atticus. Is that wise? Maybe you should buy her some tacos or something to apologize. I know for a fact that she likes carne asada with cilantro. You can buy a few extra for us to test them, just to make sure they're good enough for the detective.>

"Maybe another time. I'm ready to go home. We've had enough mayhem for one day."

CHAPTER 5

OWL
SEE YOU
DEAD FIRST

We had a fine sleep and woke up to the smells of Atticus cooking breakfast in the kitchen. He likes to make himself omelets with vegetables in them, but he always cooks up some bacon or sausage for us and sometimes there's even gravy to go on top. This morning he made us some cherrywood smoked bacon that had been cured with celery salt, and it was fine and mellow and served up with a plate of scrambled eggs.

We hounds went outside for a while, patrolled the boundaries of our property to make sure there were no squirrels around, and when we came back in Atticus was sitting at his computer, marveling at the plans of Hudson Keane and Ignacio Medina.

"Geniuses," he muttered, and he shook his head. "I really need to go back to school. The science is moving ahead so fast."

He put *Bull Durham* on Blu-Ray for us so I could teach Starbuck about the lava lizards of the Galapagos Islands and why he should never be a lollygagger. Just as Ebby Calvin LaLoosh was telling Crash Davis he wanted to "announce my presence with authority," an authority from Portland called Atticus. He paused the movie and put Detective Ibarra on speaker.

"Medina was killed in the Eugene train station, same method as Hudson Keane, a hard plastic bolt to the head. Turns out Keane had taken Medina to the Portland station to see him off."

"Where did they find him?" Atticus asked.

"They got him in the men's bathroom."

"So it wasn't the same killer. It couldn't have been."

"Well, it's theoretically possible, but he would have had to drive like hell to beat the train. And if he did that, he wouldn't have had time to come back up to Portland and ransack Keane's place before we got there. So we're talking multiple perps here."

"Where does Medina live?"

"I'm calling you from his place in East Portland. It's been tossed just like Keane's, but so far no string of numbers hidden anywhere. No damn iguanas, either, so that's a plus. Financials paint a picture very similar to Hudson's. Lots of credit card visits to coffee and donut shops—the man liked his Voodoo Doughnuts—but otherwise everything's cash."

"So someone is secretly financing two engineers but we don't know where they were working, unless it's in those coffee shops."

"Well, sort of. Turns out they were leasing an office on the second floor of the train station. We don't know why though, apart from the fact that the space is pretty cheap; there's almost nothing in it. But we'll see if we can get any camera footage of them in the coffee shops, maybe get lucky and figure out why someone wanted them dead."

We already knew why, but Atticus wasn't going to tell her that. We had to figure out who was paying Keane and Medina, and who was paying the assassins. It looked like it was going to be all about following the money, which disappointed me. Hounds aren't great at following bank transactions.

"Because they were both murdered the same day in the same way and their financials are almost identical, I don't have to use that anonymous tip someone gave me to connect them," Ibarra said. "But if you—or your anonymous source— know anything else, I'd be happy to hear it."

"I'll let you know if I find something, Detective," Atticus said. "I don't suppose you got anything from the cameras at the station?"

"Yeah, we pulled the footage but I haven't got a report from my people yet."

"Let me know when you do?"

The detective agreed and after they hung up we were able to get to the part where Crash was instructing Ebby on his clichés before the phone rang again. It was Suluk Black.

"I was going to take my time visiting you and call before I got there," she said, "but now I'm wondering if you can pick me up near Eugene. I think someone's on my tail."

"Of course, no question. Can you make it to Island Park on the east side of the Willamette River, near Springfield? We'll meet you there as soon as possible, maybe forty minutes. We'll be in an old blue Chevy truck."

Orlaith and Starbuck elected to stay and finish *Bull Durham* while I went with Atticus to pick up Suluk. There wouldn't have been much room in the cab of the truck if we all went.

And I have to admit, as much as I love Orlaith and Starbuck, it was nice for just a little while to have the window all to myself. The air rushing past my nose was cool and fresh and smelled of adventure. I may have been romanticizing a *little* bit, but I couldn't help it. When Atticus gets his jaw set and clenches his hands like that I know something's going to happen. He was driving super fast, like barely keeping the tires on the road.

<What's got your aggro turned up to eleven?> I asked him when I thought we were halfway there.

Guilt ferrets, he answered, and I knew what he meant. They're bastards. Hard to shake off once they start in on you.

<Over what?>

Over Kodiak's death. I don't want Suluk's death to be on my conscience too.

<But these guys—they're not after Suluk because of you, right?>

No, I know that intellectually. But guilt ferrets don't care about that. They latch on to your emotions anyway and bite. And since we're now on the way to pick her up, if we're too late I'm going to feel like I should have bought a faster car. Or shifted to Eugene and tried to defend her instead of pick her up. Something else than simply doing all I can right this second. That's how guilt ferrets work.

<We'll get there in time, Atticus. I have a good feeling about this.> But that good feeling slowly drained away as I started to worry maybe we wouldn't get there in time. Old Chevy trucks don't move like Camaros or Corvettes. I don't know what kind of animals are associated with worry, but they were sure chewing on me something awful. Maybe bats! They kind of fly like they're worried and I certainly worry about them when they fly near me, so that was it: Worry bats were eating at my confidence.

Island Park was situated around a bend of the Willamette River that sported an island shaped kind of like a dachshund's body. You could see the island if you followed some footpaths that took you down to the shore, but from the parking lot looking west, the river was screened by a stand of trees. There was one of those modern playground areas with plastic stuff for kids to romp around on to the north, the ground coated with rubberized asphalt to cushion their ouchies when they fell down. We really couldn't see much beyond the parking lot and playground because of the trees all around us. Suluk wasn't waiting anywhere in sight. We got out of the truck, leaving the doors open and the engine running, and Atticus called Suluk's name. The answer he got was a low buzzing noise coming from the direction of the footpath.

<What is that? An attack helicopter?>

No, not enough chop to it. I think it's—yeah, it's a drone. And there's Suluk!

<Three kinds of cat shit, Atticus! They're chasing her down with a drone? Don't those things have missiles on them?> Suluk was running toward us from the north, parallel to but not exactly on the footpath. She was running a lot faster than I thought she would, more like a pro athlete than someone who had to be super old if she knew Atticus from way back.

Not this kind. It's a spy drone, and since it's mostly plastic and I don't have line-of-sight to what isn't plastic, I can't do anything to bind it. This modern tech can be trouble.

<So what are we going to do?>

Strategic retreat. Back in the truck, and stay in the middle so Suluk can cram in.

He was already moving back to the driver's seat and I jumped in from the passenger side and tried to visualize myself as a compact model hound, like a Yorkie or a Pomeranian, very fuel efficient dogs who could live on like two Vienna sausages per day.

Atticus hopped in and slammed the door shut, and with him next to me and Suluk approaching fast, I didn't think my visualization was going to help very much—unless I was the one who got squeezed down to the size of a Vienna sausage.

We became a chorus of strained grunts when Suluk half-leapt into the truck and unintentionally smooshed us to the left like rebels in an Imperial trash compactor.

"Go!" she huffed before she even got the door closed, and Atticus peeled out of there, heading back to the road. Suluk wrestled the door shut with an "Oof!" and then took two whole quick breaths before pointing out the front window at a slick black car squealing its tires into the lot as we were going out.

"That's them! I lost them at the other end of the park but they kept tabs on me with that drone!"

Atticus noted that they had tinted windows and he couldn't see inside, but they saw Suluk in our truck—or already knew she was there. They fishtailed behind us to give chase and I didn't think we'd stay ahead very long.

<That car looks like it has a lot of horses under the hood,> I said.

It's a Dodge Charger with a Hemi engine. We don't have a prayer of outrunning it.

"How many in the car?" Atticus asked Suluk.

"Two. They're armed with those little crossbows."

"No guns?"

"Not that I've seen so far."

Atticus had us back on Main Street headed back toward the cabin. It would eventually turn into the McKenzie Highway but while we were in the city it was leading us past businesses and neighborhoods that smelled like waffles for some reason.

"Are they controlling that drone from the car or is someone else feeding them info?" Atticus asked.

"I don't know," Suluk replied.

"How do you want this to end?" Atticus said as he began to weave in and out of traffic, pressing down the horn.

"Well, the crossbow they have means it's the same guys from the train station and now they're trying to kill me for witnessing their dirty deed. The police are not an option, and I don't think they'll respond to a polite request to leave me alone."

"There's always running."

She snorted. "In this old thing?"

"No, I mean on foot. We get past town and there's all this wooded area on the right-hand side. We pull over, run in there, and just disappear."

"How about a compromise?" Suluk said, peering over her shoulder at the Charger. Her eyes narrowed the way humans do sometimes when they're ready to deliver some pain. "We run into the woods and make *them* disappear."

I turned to look at Atticus to see his reaction and his eyebrows were climbing to the sky. "You sure you want to play it like that?"

"Yes, I'm sure. These aren't people who have a legitimate beef with me. They're being paid to kill strangers and they're obviously fine with that. Best thing they can do with their lives right now is become fertilizer."

"All right." Atticus asked me to duck my head down while he checked the mirror. "They're hanging back a bit. Maybe we won't have to do this."

"They're hanging back because they have a drone and can't lose us. Once we get past the city and the road opens up they'll close the gap."

Atticus only nodded, his mouth set in a grim line.

"Can you take out the drone?" Suluk asked.

"Once we're out of the truck and in the woods, yeah," he said.

"I'll go halfsies on the assassins with you after that."

"Okay."

<What about me?> I asked. Atticus went ahead and answered me out loud, figuring Suluk wouldn't think he was crazy for talking to a hound.

"Oberon, we need you to run straight into the woods and just bark the whole time. They'll follow the sound and won't be looking for an ambush. When I pull over, we're all going out the passenger door to keep the truck between us and them. Leap over the fence and get into cover quick as you can."

Atticus did several illegal things on the road and we nearly hit or got hit several times but somehow never picked up any police pursuit. The local law enforcement must have been occupied elsewhere.

Nobody said anything until we passed the final stoplight, when Atticus broke the silence.

"How did they even find you?" he said.

"I don't know. That's one of those questions you ask later." Suluk turned to look out the back window. "Here they come."

I don't really have the trick of mirrors down but I think I saw that black Charger getting closer behind us.

"That's fine. I see where we're getting out." Atticus pointed to a dense stand of timber coming up on our right. I wish I knew what kind of trees they were but I honestly don't know what to say except that they had leaves instead of needles—just the small green buds of them, though, since we were in the earliest part of spring and the trees were kind of yawning as they woke up from winter sleep. Atticus pulled off onto the shoulder and the ride got bumpier, and he warned me to brace myself for the hard braking.

As soon as we stopped, Suluk threw open the door and pelted for the barbed wire fence. She surprised me again because she wasn't just fast for a big person, she was faster than pretty much *every* person—like Atticus when he was getting boosted from the earth.

We were already over the fence by the time the Charger stopped behind our truck and two men got out. We paused to look back at them: Both white guys with sunglasses.

"Where's the drone?" Suluk said.

"I'm sure it'll be along shortly," Atticus said. "When we got out of town it probably couldn't keep up. They'll send it in after us here."

<Hey, Atticus? I don't think those are plastic crossbows.> One of the men had a small box thingie in his hands which was probably the remote control and monitor for the drone, but the other one had ducked into the back seat for a second and came out with a gun in each hand.

"Oh, shit. Into the forest, and bark like I told you!" he said, and we took off just as a couple of shots followed us and whacked into tree trunks. I started barking while Atticus and Suluk started stripping on the run, and I understood what they were up to then. Those guys weren't going to be following two humans and a hound much longer. By the time the drone caught up they'd probably already be shifted into something else—which meant I was very shortly to be in the presence of a great big bear.

Atticus only had to take off his jacket and shirt and he was ready to go: He triggered one of those charms on his necklace that bound his shape to a great horned owl and he just sort of flew out of his pants and sandals. He flapped hard and went almost straight up into the branches of a tree where he could watch for our pursuit.

Keep going, Oberon, and keep barking, he said in my mind.

Great big bears don't fly out of pants or anything else, so Suluk had to try to run and undress at the same time, just flinging clothes onto the forest floor. I was barking and taking frequent glances over my shoulder, not really running too fast. We didn't want to lose them or make them give up. In fact, since I didn't see any pursuit, I stopped and turned around, shielding my body behind a tree trunk and peeking around to one side, woofing steadily. Suluk passed me, trying to kick free of her pants, and then a few seconds later there was a series of popping noises followed by a low grunt and a whiff of something that wasn't human anymore. My ears laid back and my tail ducked down by instinct as I turned to look: Suluk had become a Kodiak brown bear, which is not a grizzly bear, but rather the greatest and biggest of great big bears, just like Irish wolfhounds are the tallest of all hounds. She tossed her head at me once and then loped off to the side, circling back toward the road. I stayed where I was and barked some more, turning to face the edge of the woods again.

The drone was entering underneath the canopy and the two white men entered behind it, one of them with the remote and the other advancing with a gun in each hand. The remote control guy sent that drone flying straight in my direction, and I barked at it like any normal hound would until an owl descended from above and just tore it apart with its talons. The man holding the remote cursed and the man holding the guns joined in after a few seconds, and I chuffed a few times as Atticus flew into the canopy and they watched him go in slack-jawed disbelief. That's when I remembered I was supposed to keep barking, so I started up again.

But they were mad now and I was making myself a target.

"God, will you shut up, you stupid mutt!" the man with the guns shouted, and he fired a couple times in my direction. They weren't well aimed but at least one of the bullets smacked into the tree behind me and to my left. I was pretty sure that was my job—to keep them annoyed and their attention on me—so I moved my head to the other side of the trunk and kept barking.

The guy who shot at me really shouldn't have done that, though. Atticus can be fiercely protective of me at times and I think this was one of those times. While I'd been barking and they'd been cussing and shooting, he'd circled around behind them through the trees, and I saw him swooping down silently on the guy holding the guns, talons outstretched. He shifted back to human in midair so that his feet planted themselves right between the guy's shoulder blades and he went down with a squawk, holding on to only one of the guns, the other one flying out of his hand. Atticus wasted no time. Before the dude could recover or his buddy could process what happened, Atticus grabbed his head and twisted hard, snapping his neck, no fuss, no mess. Then he stood up quickly in front of the other guy, all naked so his dangly bits were kind of jiggling around, and he smiled and waved in the friendliest manner, as if he hadn't just killed someone.

"Hi," he said.

"Who the hell are you?" the drone pilot growled, tossing away his remote and balling up his fists.

"You shouldn't have shot at my hound. Or at Ignacio Medina, for that matter, or Hudson Keane. Was that you, who shot Hudson Keane in Portland?"

"What? No. We just had the job in Eugene—hey. Screw you, man."

Atticus just smiled even more widely at him. "Your buddy got the better deal. Never saw what hit him, hardly felt a thing. You're going to get torn up, though, by that bear behind you."

"Whatever, man, I'm not falling for that—" But Suluk Black charged in roaring at that point, and a genuine Kodiak roar isn't the kind of thing Atticus could manage through ventriloquism. The drone pilot turned, saw her, and screamed, having just enough time to process that those claws were going to be the end of him.

A couple weeks back, when we were saving Jack the poodle and a bunch of other hounds from a nasty human in Arkansas, the man got torn up pretty good by a much smaller bear before Atticus could call him off, because that bear was pretty angry, having just been sprayed with shotgun pellets. Well, Suluk was angrier than that, and Atticus couldn't have called her off even if he wanted to.

There's a reason I'm afraid of great big bears, and Suluk demonstrated why perfectly. Every time she took a swipe at that drone pilot, parts of him flew away—and I'm not just talking about blood. I mean chunky parts of him, like limbs or hunks of flesh like pot roasts and soon after that, internal organs. But she left his neck and head alone so he'd know what was happening and could feel it all. She didn't stop until he stopped screaming, and then she sat down on her hind legs, calm as you please, though she was breathing hard through those bellows in her chest.

"It's all right now, Oberon, if you want to come back," Atticus called. I came out from behind the tree and trotted back maybe halfway before I stopped.

<This looks like a good place to relax and wait,> I said. I really didn't want to get too close. <You have to get dressed and stuff, right?>

"And stuff, yeah," Atticus agreed. He looked over his shoulder in the direction of the road as the sound of a big eighteen-wheeler rumbled past. He couldn't see much, though, so that meant the truck driver couldn't see the carnage from the road, either.

Atticus turned over the body of the guy with the guns and searched for car keys. Once he removed them, he took a deep breath and closed his eyes, and soon after that the ground underneath the assassins started shifting. Suluk grunted in surprise and stood up, backing away. My Druid was having the Willamette elemental swallow up the bodies and assorted parts so that there'd be no evidence. I noticed that he buried the drone and the guns too.

While he was doing that, Suluk lumbered away out of sight and I heard that popping noise again. I guessed she was modest about her shifting process, which was strange because she had no problem walking around naked in front of Atticus. She strolled back to check on his progress, her hands a bit bloodstained, and when the ground stopped moving and Atticus opened his eyes, she nodded at him once.

"Thanks," she said, and he tossed her the keys, which she snatched out of the air. "Huh. New car. Thanks again."

"It's later now," Atticus said, "so let's ask that question again. How did these guys find you? Who the hell are they?"

Suluk shrugged. "No idea."

"The killer in that stairwell didn't get a good look at you, right?"

"He probably saw me okay, but it wasn't for very long, and he certainly didn't snap a picture."

"Oh. A picture! That has to be it. Not good, though."

"I don't follow."

"I'm still piecing it together, so I'm thinking aloud. You said these guys had those plastic crossbows, right? We'll find them in the car?"

"Yeah."

"So they're related somehow to that Portland murder. And they wouldn't have reason to go after you except that you witnessed it, right?"

"Right."

"Well, clearly these are high tech guys with their weapons and their drones. It's easy to see how they tracked you once they found you. But if you're an anonymous bystander, how did they find you? And the answer is surveillance footage."

"From the train station?"

"At first, yes. You're under surveillance almost anywhere you go in a city these days. You're on camera forty, fifty times a day, easy, just walking around town. So they take a screen cap of your face in the train station, run it through facial recognition software, and then start running searches for a match. That's how they found you in Eugene."

"Shit. But that means some serious stalking. And resources."

"That's right. But they have to have access to the train station footage to begin with. And who had that?"

Suluk swore again. "The cops."

"Exactly. Someone in the Portland P.D. is helping."

"Well, I'd like to stuff a whale down their cheesehole."

I'd never heard of that particular hole before. I'd have to ask Atticus how humans were managing to keep them hidden if you could insert whole whales into them.

"You'd better just go. Take their car and get out of here. Disappear for a few months in the woods. If you stay away from cameras and don't have a human face to recognize, you'll be in the clear."

Suluk nodded. "All right. I'll go to the Strawberry Mountain Wilderness in Malheur National Park, somewhere around Strawberry Lake."

"Good."

"But after I get dressed."

CHAPTER 6

THERE ARE RULES ABOUT TACOS

Once Suluk drove off to the east in the Charger, Atticus called Detective Ibarra and asked if he could buy her tacos for lunch. She gave him an address and he said we'd meet her there in an hour. We drove back to the cabin, fixed up a snack for Starbuck and Orlaith, and then we shifted to the Japanese Garden in Washington Park where Atticus had bound a tree. We had to jog from there to 16th and NW Northrup in the Pearl District, where there was a taco cart that the detective claimed had the best tacos in Portland.

It was called Frogtown Tacos, and they made their tortillas fresh right in front of you on a hot grill thingie. Atticus bought a huge mess of carne asada tacos, four of them just for me, and asked that they leave off the onions on mine. We took them back to the detective's tiny car and the humans sat on the hood and chowed down while I properly wolfed down my tacos once Atticus unwrapped them for me. They were so delicious and I had to make sure she knew I appreciated it.

<Atticus, you need to tell Detective Ibarra she has fantastic taste. I think she's all right and it's probably okay to call her Gabriela now.>

Uh, no, buddy, I don't think she'd appreciate being called by her first name. We don't have that kind of relationship.

That confused me. <Humans can share amazing tacos with someone and spill stuff out the ends and stain their clothing yet still maintain formal relationships? I thought sharing tacos automatically meant you were friends.>

I wish the world worked that way, but it doesn't.

<Well, at least tell her she knows good food!>

"You're right, Detective," Atticus said around a mouthful. "These are the best tacos in Portland."

"Right?" she said, her mouth also full. She smacked her lips a couple of times and waved a hand around at the intersection. "I mean, it's got shit for seating, I know, but you can't beat the quality."

"Well, I've got shit for details, but you can't beat the tip I have for you."

"Oh yeah? What's that?"

"Someone working the case in your department is taking money from the same people who paid to have Keane and Medina killed. You have a corrupt cop on your force."

Detective Ibarra stopped chewing and glared at Atticus in silence for a few decades. He did not appear concerned—in fact, he made me proud by stuffing half a taco into his face, showing that he had no intention of elaborating on that no matter how dirty a look she gave him. When she raised one eyebrow at him in an attempt to make him talk, he just raised one of his eyebrows in return, his cheeks puffed out like a chipmunk. She shook her head, finished chewing, and dabbed at her mouth with a paper napkin before saying anything more.

"On what evidence are you basing this accusation?"

Atticus took a moment to clear his mouth before saying, "I can't share that. Sorry."

"Well, you have to give me something. I can't investigate a colleague without cause."

"You know what these murders are about?"

She shrugged. "Money would be my guess."

"Mine too. Specifically, money from the energy industry."

"How do you know that? Did you figure out something from those numbers I gave you?"

"No," Atticus lied. "Just deductive reasoning. Ignacio Medina was an electrical engineer and Hudson Keane was a chemical engineer. Put those facts together with their secret bankrolling and they were probably working on breakthrough solar tech, which would create lots of enemies. Autocratic nations who depend on oil would be threatened, let alone multinational corporations."

"Plausible, sure. But you're withholding something from me."

"I withhold plenty from you and you've known that from the first day we met. I freely admit that I occasionally dabble in matters beyond dog training. But I hope you also know I'm trying to help you. Look, it doesn't matter to me if you charge your colleague with this or that. You can keep it all hush-hush so long as he talks. He's not the priority. Following the money is, because whoever paid off your cop will lead you to who's behind the murders of Hudson Keane and Ignacio Medina."

"Well, I think we already have at least one of our murderers on tape. Want to see?"

"Sure." She ducked into her car for a moment and fetched a tablet, then returned to sit next to Atticus on the hood. I positioned myself so I could get a look too, and Atticus helped make it look natural by petting my head.

The video was one of those black-and-white security feeds with numbers flickering in the corner, which Atticus called timecode and which meant I'd never have a chance of understanding it.

It was a shot of the Portland train station platform with a bunch of humans milling about as the train left the station. The detective pointed to a couple of them. "There," she said. "That's your lookalike, Hudson Keane. That woman right there, see her?" She paused the video to get a freeze frame. "She clearly knows him. They're talking and smiling. She walks with him into the station, into that stairwell, and then a few minutes later, she walks back out with her hood up. Looks Native American, maybe."

"Maybe," Atticus said, but he could do better than that. She was of the Alutiiq people who live in the Kodiak archipelago and he knew it, because we were looking at none other than Suluk Black.

<Hey! Why's she all buddy-buddy with him? I thought she said she chased after Hudson because she thought he was you?>

She did, Oberon. She flat-out lied to us. She knew him all along and also knew I wasn't dead. To the detective he said, "Was she the only person to go into that stairwell with him or come out?"

"No. There's someone else who goes in and comes out we can't identify at all. Look." She let the video play again and pointed to someone going into the stairwell after Suluk and Hudson wearing a balaclava and sunglasses. That fit the description of the murderer that Suluk gave us, at least.

"Whoever that is looks pretty shady," Atticus said.

"Yeah, but the problem is, we have no way to trace that person, and there's no obvious display of the weapon on either of them. What we have to do is find the woman Keane was talking to, because she either committed the murder or witnessed it."

"How long have you had this video?"

"Me personally? A couple hours, maybe. Just got around to it."

"But the department pulled the video long before that, right?"

"Yeah. Why?"

"Like I said, someone in your department is dirty. You need to take a look at whoever saw this video before you, and follow the money from there."

"Connor, wait," she said, and don't think I didn't notice she used his first name. She knew the rules about tacos and friendship even if Atticus didn't. "Do you know who this woman is?"

Atticus shrugged. "I might know somebody who does. Make you a deal, Detective. I'll try to track her down for you, and you look into your department for me. Somebody had to make a big cash deposit in the last couple of days." He thrust out his hand for her to shake and she considered a moment before taking him up on it.

"Wonder if I'm making a deal with the devil," she said.

"Nah, no worries about that, Detective. The devil would never be interested in animal rights."

"Huh. You probably have a point there. What's your hound's name again? Oberon?" I perked up at the mention.

"Yeah, that's right."

"Think he'll let me pet him?"

I didn't wait for Atticus to say yes. I just wagged my tail and walked around to her so she could get to it.

"Ha! I think you have your answer, Detective."

She gave me some scritches and told me I was a very good boy, then she looked up at Atticus. "You know, Connor, when it's just us like this, you can call me Gabby."

<Aha! You see, Atticus? I was right! It's always first names after tacos! There are rules!>

CHAPTER 7

STRAWBERRY FIELDS FOR A YEAR

Atticus isn't perfect but he likes to think he is. He doesn't like to be taken for a fool, but whenever it happens, he mutters a lot. After saying farewell to his new friend Gabby, he repeated in stunned disbelief, "Suluk lied to me. What the hell." And endless variations of that.

We jogged back to the bound tree in Washington Park and paused there while he got out his cell phone and called Suluk.

"Great timing," she said. "I'm about to drift out of tower range."

"Where are you?"

"I'm in Burns. Getting ready to ditch the car and walk into the National Forest."

"We need to talk. Meet you at the lake in an hour?"

"Sure."

We shifted home after that and checked in with Starbuck and Orlaith. Granuaile was home from her bartending job in Poland—she shifts around the world every day because she's trying to build a Polish headspace. She was super tired and ready to sleep, though, so we didn't talk very much. Orlaith was happy, though, her tail wagging.

<Are we going to nap together?> she asked her Druid. <I could go for a tandem napping session right about now.>

"It's a deal," Granuaile said. Both of our Druids understand that napping is a team sport.

Starbuck wanted to go with us to the lake, however, so the three of us shifted there to an old lodgepole pine Atticus had bound a long time ago.

The squirrels in the neighborhood were properly respectful of us and ran away without argument or throwing their nuts around, unlike those city squirrels. The lake itself was very pretty, resting in a little valley beneath Strawberry Mountain, which did not look like a strawberry at all. We had it all to ourselves; it was still pretty cold outside and few hikers were willing to brave such weather.

Suluk had no problem with it, though. She walked up some time later after Starbuck and I had explored the whole perimeter of the lake. We were waiting for her on the side where Atticus said she'd be coming from, in the direction of the trailhead.

She waved at us and was smiling until she got a good look at Atticus. "What's wrong?"

"You knew who Hudson Keane was the whole time. You lied to me."

Her shoulders slumped and her mouth twisted in remorse. "Yeah, I did. I'm sorry. I was scared."

"You knew Ignacio Medina too."

"Yeah, I did. I was the one funding their research."

"You were the source of all those cash deposits?"

She nodded, her mouth a tight line of regret. "I never really wanted to do what Dad was doing, managing accounts for people like you. When he went roaming as a bear, it was me who looked after things, you know."

"Yeah, I knew that."

"Well, that meant we could never go roaming together, you know? When I was young—I mean the seventeenth century, back before the Russian fur traders came and wrecked our culture—we used to go to the salmon runs together every year and have the best time eating fresh fish out of the Karluk River, or wherever else we went. But as the decades ticked past, he wound up having so many clients that it became a full-time job to just keep up with things. One or the other of us always had to be human. So a couple years back I suggested this project to him as a way to keep ourselves flush but get out of the long-term accounting business. Riding high on an energy innovation would keep us rolling in money forever without having to do much day-to-day. Dad agreed and we hooked up with Iggy and Hudson. And when he got killed, well, I just kept going with it. I've let all the accounting clients go. This was my shot, but I don't have their research notes, so now it's toast."

"Maybe not," Atticus said. "Tell me why Iggy was going to Eugene. You both went to see him off, right?"

"Yeah. He was heading down to check on a prototype installation we had set up, inspect for degradation, record energy output and efficiency, that sort of thing."

"After Hudson got killed, didn't you call to warn him?"

Suluk nodded. "I did! I did. As soon as I was out of the train station." She dashed a tear away from the corner of her eye and sniffed. "But it didn't do any good. They were waiting for him at the other end. He was supposed to call me back when he was safe, but he never did. When I called again to check up on him, I got a message that his number was out of service. They destroyed his phone."

"Who did this? Who are 'they'?"

"Someone who either wants to prevent their tech from getting to market or someone who wants to steal it. Take your pick. How'd you find out? Did the police discover the lab?"

"No. Not as far as I know, anyway. They showed me security footage from the train station. They have a clear shot of your face and saw you enter that stairwell with Hudson. They want to talk to you."

"I really don't want to do that. They're going to dig around in my business and find out I'm four hundred years old."

"Four hundred? Wow."

"Never mind that. They're going to freeze my assets and take my DNA and figure out I'm not entirely human. I can't let them do that."

"Why not? You haven't committed any murders they can pin on you, right?"

Suluk just stared at Atticus and said nothing, but she didn't have to. It wasn't hard to guess that those bodies back in the forest weren't the first that Suluk had put down, and they wouldn't be the last. "Oh. Okay, then. No DNA," my Druid said, and walked over to the shore. He picked up a flat rock and skipped it across the surface of the water six times, showing off his opposable thumbs. Suluk joined him and skipped her rock seven times.

"Speaking of DNA, Hudson was my great-great-grandson."

"No kidding? No wonder he looked like you. Did you know?"

"No, I hadn't a clue. I'd go mad if I tried to have a relationship with my descendants."

"I understand. I have a few different lines of descent myself. You get lonely and it hurts too much so you let yourself love for a while, but it's like getting drunk. Feels real good for a time but the hangover's waiting on the other side. Kids, I mean. Except they don't go away if you take two aspirin. Couldn't tell you what happened to most of them. I only keep in touch with the one who got to be a bear. He's up in British Columbia, trying to start his own family right now."

"That's great."

"Sure is." Suluk picked up another rock and tossed it at the lake, but she must have lost her Zen mojo or something, because it just plunked in without skipping at all. "What did you mean when you said maybe my plan isn't toast after all?"

"Hudson had his research stored on an encrypted flash drive. I found it in his place and decrypted it. Snuck it out of there right under the cops' noses."

I expected some jumping up and down at that point or maybe a fist pump on Suluk's part, but she stood very still, didn't even turn her head. She looked out at the lake and the silence grew. I laid down in the grass between them and Starbuck crawled on top of me and sprawled across my back, sighing a spluttery sort of sigh.

"What do you want?" Suluk finally said.

"I want you to tell me why you didn't have a copy of this already. And then I want in."

Suluk grunted. "We had an informal agreement. They needed my money and I needed their brains. They wanted to keep their research secret because most scientists get ripped off these days by the corporations that employ them. I said I'd agree to that if they followed a strict security discipline regarding their money and in going to the lab so no one would realize what we were up to. The research was going well and we were just about ready to file for incorporation and a patent, take everything from informal to formal. That office space above the train station was going to be our front. We were going to split the patent up four ways."

"Four ways?"

"Dad was going to be the fourth."

"Oh. Well, it can all still happen. Make me the fourth. Make Hudson and Iggy's families the other beneficiaries. Or not. Your call. In the meantime, I can make the police go away."

Suluk's head moved ever so slightly in his direction. "How?"

"Let me record a video of your testimony, like an affidavit. And give me someone to go after."

"I don't know who's doing this. I don't even know how anyone found out about the project. Either Iggy or Hudson screwed up somehow and let it leak."

"We have to prove someone else committed the murders or you can never live in the open again. You'll always be a suspect because of the security footage."

"I know. But I honestly haven't the slightest clue who's after us."

Atticus sighed. "We'll have to hope Detective Ibarra can come up with something, then."

CHAPTER 8

MURDER
BY DELIVERY

I have to admit that humans are pretty funny when they get self-conscious. Point a camera at them and they instantly start worrying about how they look. They make a fuss about their hair, usually, but their greatest fear is that there might be a tiny little booger hanging out in their nostrils. Suluk Black was no different, even though she was a great big bear and could tear apart anyone who made fun of her boogers. Once Atticus pointed a camera at her, she became a wreck until Atticus reminded her that she was four hundred years old and she should have oodles of dignity and gravitas—things that I didn't realize came in oodles until he said it.

Atticus had shifted into town to get the camera with a memory card in it and came back to film Suluk in front of Strawberry Lake. She wouldn't give her name, or even any of her actual aliases, but made up a new one instead. She was "the Marmot," a secretive financier of scientific research who paid scientists in cash and operated in the shadows to foil the efforts of corporate espionage. She admitted to financing the solar research of Hudson Keane and Ignacio Medina and recounted what happened in the stairwell, but refused to come in to the police for questioning. She ended by stating her fervent hope that the police would catch the killers of two brilliant young minds.

"That's great," Atticus said as he turned off the camera. "They won't give up on you with this, but at least they'll entertain other possibilities. They'll waste time searching for the Marmot though, and that cracks me up."

Suluk had a cave up in the Strawberry Mountain Wilderness somewhere and she was going to be a bear for a while, but check back at the lake every day to see if Atticus was there and needed to talk. They agreed to work on the solar business after the murders were cleared up—or at least, Hudson's. We were pretty sure the murderers of Ignacio Medina had been buried outside Eugene, but Suluk wasn't a suspect in that one. Unless...

<Hey, Atticus. After we leave, I have to run an idea by you to make sure we aren't chasing our tails here.>

Okay, buddy. We said farewell to Suluk and shifted back to the cabin. "What's the big idea?" he said aloud.

<Just making sure: What if Suluk was the one who paid the mercenaries to kill Hudson and Iggy so she could have the

solar tech all for herself? She would have a financial motive, and by having Hudson killed when she was around she'd throw suspicion off herself.>

"Those murders weren't Suluk's style. If she wanted someone dead, no one would ever find the body. They'd just disappear. No body means no murder investigation, and no investigation means no contact with the police. That's her highest priority."

<Oh, yeah, I see that now.>

"It's good you're being thorough."

<What's next?>

"Popcorn and apples and a movie. We'll get this video to Detective Ibarra in the morning and see if she's made any progress on her end. What movie shall we watch?"

Is it okay if we watch Hellboy? *I was telling Orlaith about Sammael the Desolate One, Hound of Resurrection, and how the movie completely ignores physics like the squirrel on the train did, so she wants to see it.*

Orlaith was immensely comforted to learn that creatures from hell regularly ignored physics and that therefore squirrels must be from hell, which only confirmed our long-held suspicions. The world made sense again.

In the morning Granuaile had already gone back to Poland and Orlaith wanted to come with us, so we drove all the way to Portland since we'd woken too late to catch the train. It was close enough to lunchtime when we got there that Detective Ibarra agreed to meet us in Beaverton at a Vietnamese place called Phở King Good, the name of which Atticus found amusing. The phở was indeed quite good: He bought bowls of brisket phở to go for us hounds and asked them to leave out the green onion. He and the detective sat on the curb and ate theirs next to us and did one of those *squid pro go* thingies.

Atticus gave her the memory card from the camera and pretended he had gotten it from someone else. "My guy found the woman from the security footage and got her to record a statement. Not sure how much it will help."

"If it doesn't help enough I'm going to need your contact and talk to her in person."

"Let's hope it helps enough, then, because I doubt she can be found unless she wants to. The Marmot stays off the grid as much as possible. It's amazing she let herself be filmed in the train station."

"The Marmot?"

"Shadowy figure, sort of like Keyser Söze except she's involved in underground science instead of drugs."

"You're messing with me, right?"

"No, it's true."

"Damn, just when I thought I'd heard everything. Well, you were right about someone being on the take. Remember that footage I showed you yesterday of this Marmot person in the train station? He smuggled out a picture of her before I even had a look at it."

<So that's how Suluk had people tailing her so quickly!> I said.

Yep. But they still had to identify her and track her down. That means some pretty serious resources.

"So you found him because he made a big cash deposit."

"Yeah. Though he was trying to be smart about it by making smaller deposits, any cash deposit over a couple hundred bucks for a cop is going to raise some questions. Gave me a line about selling off a coin collection, but he had no proof of sale and he didn't like the idea of being tied to the murder. He decided to help instead."

"Are you going to charge him?" Atticus said.

"I haven't decided yet. He's dirty for sure, but you can't snitch on another cop without consequences."

"How did he get the picture out?"

Detective Ibarra held up the memory card Atticus gave her. "Like this, actually. He froze a frame of the footage, took a picture of it with a digital camera, removed the card, and made the handoff."

"A live handoff?"

"Right in front of the station, too. Gigantic balls, eh?"

"So you have tape on that, I bet."

"Yes, we do. But we can't really prove anything. The video's useless."

"How so?"

"He was told to pick up a delivery of pizza and wings at a certain time. Delivery guy rides up on a scooter and he's covered head to toe in winter gear, and the license plate is 'accidentally' covered up as well. My dirty cop has the memory card folded up inside a couple of twenties for the driver so you can't see him making any illegal exchange. And inside the bag of wings is actually a couple of fat stacks of bills for him."

"But there was really pizza and wings in there too?"

"Yeah."

"So the pizza place is going to have a record of that delivery! Gabby, we can nail the driver and—" Atticus didn't finish because the detective was shaking her head.

"Already tried that. This place is called Pisa Pizza and none of their locations have a record of a delivery to the station this week. Someone picked it up, paid cash, and then made the delivery. We're trying to figure out who that was now by going through the pizza place's tapes and matching orders for pizza and wings to faces. But it's just due diligence. Nothing will come of it. Even if we can match a nameless customer face to the order, it won't help because we can't match that face to the anonymous delivery guy. And before you ask, we also asked if any of their drivers use a scooter. No luck."

"Damn."

<Hey now, wait a second, Atticus. This isn't fitting together right.>

What do you mean, Oberon? he asked me mind-to-mind.

<This person in the winter clothes. They were at the train station. And they were also at the apartment complex, right? And then making this pizza delivery on a scooter.>

Yeah, so?

<So remember you said there was a camera at the apartment complex pointed at the parking lot? What was the killer driving then? A scooter or something else?>

Whoa, good catch, Oberon. Let me ask. He jerked his head around as if he'd just been struck by an idea and said, "Gabby, did you ever look at the footage from the parking lot?"

"Keane's place? Yeah. Perp was driving an older model white Corolla with stolen plates from Kansas."

"So not a scooter, then?"

"No. That's a good point! We might be dealing with more than one person here."

"Or the same person who is very careful to use a different vehicle for every crime, knowing how easy they are to trace."

"We'll check the clothing and posture and so on to see if it's the same person or not."

<Atticus, we should go to this pizza place and use our noses.>

You just ate, Oberon.

<I'm not talking about food this time! Maybe for the first time, I admit, but look: if it *is* the same person in all these tapes and they've been to the pizza place, Starbuck might be able to pick up the scent. Because he connected them in the stairwell and at the apartment.>

It's worth a try, he said to me privately, then turned to Gabby. "Which location would have delivered to the station? You have an address?"

"Yeah. Why?"

Atticus used his thumb to point at us. "Because the science of olfaction might still apply here. If the delivery dude was the same person who ransacked Keane's apartment they might be able to pick up his scent. And the person who ransacked the apartment was the one who pulled the trigger at the train station."

The detective turned to consider us. "That's going to be a paper-thin case. I don't know how I can prove they smelled the right guy. Or explain why we're stalking Pisa Pizza without exposing my crooked colleague."

"I'm sure we'll figure something out if we have to. Let's just see what they can smell. Might be nothing."

"Or it might be everything."

"Won't know unless we try."

The humans finished up their phở and got everything thrown away before the detective looked up the address. She said she'd meet us there and drove separately. It took us twenty years to pull into the parking lot of a strip mall that featured a nail salon, a laundromat, and a tax preparation service in addition to Pisa Pizza. Altogether it smelled of ethyl acetate, perfumed detergent, pepperoni, and existential despair. Atticus leashed us up and asked privately that we let Starbuck lead on this, and also to ignore the stupid things he would say out loud to make it seem to the detective like we were trained scent hounds and not able to understand his speech.

Heading up to the place I wasn't sure that Starbuck or any hound could pick out a human smell over all the meat and cheese, and when the little guy said, <Yes food!> I thought the trip was a bust. But Atticus pressed the Boston to make sure.

Do you mean yes you smell food or yes you smell the man we're looking for? Evidently it was both; he might not have all his words yet, but he could still tell Atticus things through non-verbal cues and feelings. *Starbuck says the scent is strong. Not just on the ground but all around the door jamb.* Atticus looked at the detective.

"He was here. No doubt about it." He peered through the glass of the door to the interior and I followed his gaze. There was a counter with a register and a menu hanging above it showing delicious pies made of fat and grease. To the left of the counter there was a gap leading into the kitchen area for employees. "I want to go in and check on something," he said. "Back me up that these are service dogs?"

"Okay, sure, but wait—"

Atticus didn't wait. He pulled open the door and told Starbuck to follow that scent. No sooner did he cross the threshold than the manager called out a challenge. She was middle-aged, I think, had her hair pulled back into a ponytail hanging out the back of a baseball cap, and she looked and sounded tired.

"Sir? You can't bring dogs in here. It's against the health code."

Starbuck ignored her and pulled to the left, short snout tracking along the floor, his nose full of bad guy. He headed straight for that gap in the counter rather than the cash register, where customers would go. The manager got louder the closer we got to the kitchen and moved to intercept us. Atticus told us to hold up before we started an imbroglio—that's a word that you can pull out most anywhere and expect someone to give you brownie points or sometimes an actual brownie.

He turned to Detective Ibarra and said, "He works here. We'll wait outside."

We headed back for the door as the detective flashed her badge at the manager. "Portland Homicide. We have reason to believe one of your employees is involved in a murder."

"You've gotta be shitting me," the manager said. "This is all I need."

I didn't hear the detective's answer to that because the door closed behind us after that and Atticus congratulated us on being awesome.

"Only a matter of time, now," he said. "We are about to solve another crime and it's all thanks to the best hounds anywhere. Negotiations for a special meal are now open."

<Chicken fried steak with gravy!> Orlaith suggested.

<Shredded beef brisket poutine!> I said because I figured we would win either way.

<Yes food!> Starbuck added. He's not picky yet.

The detective brought out a series of sullen teenagers one by one to see if any of them matched the scent of the killer. Starbuck snuffled at each greasy hand but none of them matched. The detective was bringing the manager to the door just as a car drove up with a Pisa Pizza sign attached to the top of it by a magnet. Atticus was paying attention to the detective and the manager coming to the door, so he didn't see the car or the guy who got out of it.

He was pretty tall and ripped for a delivery guy. He looked like he could be a bouncer or a bodyguard and make lots more money that way, just flexing at smaller people and intimidating them. He was a white guy who had his hair cut the way white supremacists do: short on the sides and a small lawn of dark limp hair on the top. I barked almost by reflex because ever since World War Two, Atticus has lived by the moral code that "if you see a Nazi, punch a Nazi," and this guy set off my alarm bells. That car of his was white too.

<Whoa, Atticus, have Starbuck check out this dude.>

Atticus didn't even have to ask because Starbuck sensed him coming and turned to investigate. His wee nose snuffled and twitched in the air as the detective pushed open the door and the guy said, "Excuse me," since we were kind of blocking the entrance. Atticus automatically started to move out of the way and the detective held the door open as Starbuck planted himself and started barking like five cats had stolen all his fish sticks. <No squirrel!> he shouted, but Atticus got more sense out of him than that.

"It's him," he told the detective, and things happened pretty fast after that.

"Detective Ibarra," she said, and pulled out her badge. "Portl-uggh!" Lightning fast, the dude socked her in the nose before she could finish and straight-kicked Atticus in the gut, knocking him down and thereby jerking our leashes in the process. Then he took off—but not to his car, which surprised me. He was headed for the other end of the strip mall, where I guess he hoped to turn the corner. There must be an alley back there or someplace he thought he could hide.

Bring him down, Atticus said in our heads, and let go of our leashes. *But don't break the skin.*

The dude was pretty fast for a human but he was slower than a box turtle on barbiturates compared to three hounds. We caught up to him in front of the nail salon. Starbuck and I nipped at his heels and tripped him up. He fell sprawling on the concrete and Orlaith just kept running right over him, making sure to plant a foot on the back of his head and ram his chin into the sidewalk. But once she was off him and past, he kicked out at me and Starbuck, tagging both of us, though it didn't hurt much—it just pushed us back and gave him room to gain his feet. Atticus wasn't having any of that; the guy would probably be able to aim a much better kick from a standing position. I heard Atticus mumble something in Old

Irish—he was making a binding of some kind—and Detective Ibarra was telling him to freeze.

You can back away, I've got him now, Atticus said, and I saw what he meant. The guy took exactly one step and then the inseams of his jeans fused together as he tried to take another and he fell down again, growling in his frustration. He flopped like a professional soccer player but then Detective Ibarra fell on him with a knee in his back, pinning him. She had him in cuffs a few seconds later and Atticus undid the binding on his jeans.

Good job, you three, Atticus told us in our heads. *Where did he think he was going?*

I trotted to the corner and looked past the mall. There was one of those alleys where trucks could make deliveries, but then there was a low wall he could have jumped over and he'd be in an apartment complex. Lots of places to hide in there and lose us.

<He might have made it if he could have gotten over the wall back there,> I said. <No way he could have lost us in the car once the detective made him. It was probably his best move. But it just wasn't good enough against the Hounds of the Willamette and their pet Druid!>

...Pet Druid? Really?

<Don't complain, now, you know we take good care of you.>

The detective smooshed the perp's face into the concrete with one hand because he was calling her some rather unkind names, and used her other hand to fish a wallet out of his back pocket. She flipped it open and read the name on the driver's license. She sniffed before talking because she had a bloody nose.

"Brock Slater, you're under arrest for assaulting a police officer," she said. "And we'll see what we can add on to that later."

The manager of Pisa Pizza came over and put her hands on her hips. "Now I've gotta do all the deliveries tonight. You're fired, Brock. You asshole."

I didn't think that was enough. You can't kick me, Starbuck, and Atticus and punch our taco friend, Gabby, and just get handcuffed and fired. I remembered Atticus's rule about Nazis and realized he couldn't follow through on that now; Gabby wouldn't allow stuff like that. But I could modify Atticus's rule and get away with it. I trotted over to him and lifted my leg on his head. I have pretty good aim. Gabby reared back just in time so none of it got on her.

Oberon, what are you doing? Atticus sounded horrified.

<If you see a Nazi, pee on a Nazi,> I said. <I'm modifying your rule to match my particular skill set.>

Brock Slater made grunting noises and swore a lot and demanded Gabby do something because I had a half liter or gallon or whatever to unload on him and it was taking a while.

"I'd love to help, but I'm fully occupied just keeping you restrained. I'll tell him he's a bad dog, though." She grinned at me, which Slater couldn't see. "Bad dog, Oberon."

She is totally going to buy me some tacos later, I can tell.

CHAPTER 9

GONE SQUIRREL

I thought for the longest time that chicken-fried steak was steak that had been fried by specially trained chickens, and as such was one of the rarest delicacies on the planet. You can imagine my epic disappointment when I learned that chickens weren't involved in the preparation at all—not even as part of the ingredients! Humans just fried up steak the same way they fried chicken, using a batter with secret herbs and spices. I felt sure that one of the secret herbs had to be ground-up chicken bits because why else would they be advertising that it's chicken-fried, but no, Atticus said, it was just another example of the English language being stupid sometimes, and chicken bits wouldn't count as an herb in any case. When I asked him about the bottles of spices called Poultry Seasoning he had in his pantry, he explained that it was seasoning *for* poultry, not seasoning *made of* poultry. That was a sad day of shattered illusions and disappointment with language, let me tell you, and Orlaith suffered almost the same heartbreak when she got her reward for fighting crime, because she thought chicken-fried steak meant the steak would be fried *inside* a chicken. Gravy on top made it better, of course, but I also tried to soothe her with a weird English thing that was a pleasant surprise.

<You know humans sometimes eat this stuff they call surf and turf?>

<That doesn't sound very good,> she said.

<I know! But it's a trick because they don't actually eat either one! It's a code phrase for steak and lobster. They *say* it's because cows live on turf and lobsters swim in the surf, but who are they kidding? They just like to rhyme.>

We were feeling pretty smug and Atticus said that was okay because we'd earned it. "Brock Slater had thought of everything but hounds. We never would have found him if it weren't for your noses. And that squirrel on the train."

<What? We have to share credit with a squirrel?> I said, and Orlaith protested too.

<That's not right; the squirrel didn't help at all!> and for once, when Starbuck said, <No squirrel!> it made perfect sense in context. Atticus just laughed at us.

"I only meant we wouldn't have run into that stairwell and gotten involved if it weren't for that squirrel. I'm not saying the squirrel did anything helpful. I know you did all the work."

We calmed down after that, and I admitted that the detective had done quite a bit as well, especially after handcuffing Slater. Once she got a warrant to search his home, they found a 3D printer, two plastic crossbows and plenty of bolts. There was also a bag of cash and a dossier on Hudson Keane in his kitchen, plus clothing that matched the outfit the killer wore. His car make and model matched the surveillance video of Keane's apartment complex even if the license plate did not. Atticus said it was a circumstantial case but about as strong a one as you could hope for. Strong enough that Brock Slater was willing to confess and give what information he could about who paid him for some kind of leniency on his sentence. He wasn't a professional ex-military hit man who'd die before he talked; he was "more of a punk-ass nihilist," Atticus said, who thought he'd never get caught as long as he kept his face off the cameras, and he had no code of honor or sense of loyalty to whoever hired him. I am not sure how punk asses differ from regular asses and I don't have a clue what a nihilist is either. I confess I didn't ask Atticus to explain because sometimes his explanations are short and sometimes they are college lectures. Maybe a nihilist is someone who thinks "the end is nigh" so it's okay to kill people for money. And it's okay to rat out your buddies afterward, too: Slater gave up the names of the two guys who killed Ignacio Medina in Eugene and who also came after Suluk Black. I guess they were nihilists too.

Detective Ibarra reported that Slater said, "They were supposed to find the woman who saw me do Keane, but I haven't heard back." He never would, and we couldn't help the police find those two guys without getting in trouble ourselves.

The confession made the detective very happy because she didn't need to worry about things like who the Marmot was or reveal that there was a crooked cop involved in the investigation. She was going to make him donate all the money to charity and tell him to keep his nose clean—which only reinforced my belief that clean noses are truly an obsession with humans.

And since we'd helped her clean another murder off her books, Detective Ibarra was quite happy with us in general and decided maybe that Atticus was a guy she could trust to do the right thing. She told Atticus next time the tacos were on her, and I knew we were solid then. I was so excited about future tacos I almost missed out on some of the unfinished business.

Slater didn't have the name of his client but he shared every detail of how contact was made and how the money was delivered. He also gave up information on a whole bunch of other stuff he'd done since his position as a pizza delivery guy allowed him to go anywhere without suspicion. He did the occasional drug run or money drop for shady guys while delivering pies. The detective would follow up on that because it wasn't something we could really help with, and Atticus said we'd done enough by solving the murders. He and Suluk could start Stable Solar and Battery now, and he was so pleased with us that he was going to take us to Portland again to smell all the things since we never got to do it properly the first time. He also promised to take us to a place that had oxtail poutine on the menu, and we were ready to get on board for that. Except for the fact that the squirrel got away at the start, I thought the proverbial biscuits had landed once again on the side of justice and gravy. And I knew that one day, that squirrel would get his justice too.

EPILOGUE

A couple of days later, we arrived in the Eugene train station to begin our Portland Smelling Expedition and there was a squirrel on top of the train *again!* It might have even been the same squirrel as before! What if he was a commuter?

<Okay Atticus, you have to admit this time that something weird is going on! This is not normal behavior!>

<No squirrel!> Starbuck said.

All right, all right. I'll admit that it's unusual. If you want to find out what's happening, I'll help this time. But you have to behave strangely too if this is going to work.

<How do you mean?>

If we get to Portland and he hasn't been destroyed by physics, we'll follow him. But you can't bark at him and tip him off that he's being tailed. We have to be sneaky about it. Think you can do that?

<You want us *not* to bark at a squirrel?> Orlaith said. <That's beyond strange. That's unnatural.>

I agreed with Orlaith and said so. <We might be crossing a line here, Atticus.>

It's the squirrel who's crossed the line, he argued. *And if you want to get to the bottom of this, you're going to have to cross a line too. I'll tap into his noggin and keep tabs on him so even if he ducks around a corner we won't lose him, okay?*

Orlaith and I weren't too sure about the plan but decided to try it in the end. Barking sure felt good—it felt *right*—but it hadn't worked up to that point, so maybe it was time to try a new strategy.

You'll be stealth hounds, Atticus said, and that made us feel a little better about not barking. It was stealth technology.

We got onto the train camouflaged as before and were quiet like before, and Atticus didn't have any trouble with the train staff. But once we got to Portland and stepped out on the platform, we looked up at the roof of the train and saw that squirrel, smug as a frat boy who got a deal on a keg of cheap beer.

<You see him, Atticus? I see him and I'm not barking.>

<Me neither, but it's really hard,> Orlaith said. Starbuck made a low growl in his throat but didn't bark. We reminded him we were going stealth and he stopped.

I see him and I'm binding to him now, Atticus said. *Even if he dips out of sight I won't lose him. Let's just follow at a safe distance.*

The little poufy rat scrambled along the top of the train and jumped to the roof of the platform canopy before shimmying down the post just like he had before. But he took a different route after that, leading us out of the station, slipping out a door behind someone who was unconscious of him being there.

Huh. I'm starting to think something's up, Atticus said.

<Only now you're starting to think that? Well, better late than never, I guess.>

This isn't a random search for food. The squirrel has a destination in mind. He's moving with purpose.

Orlaith said, <We've been trying to explain to you and Granuaile that they *always* have a sinister purpose, but you never believe us.>

Well, a purpose and a sinister purpose are very different things. Let's wait and see.

<Can't you find out what the purpose is?> I asked.

Not without alerting him that I'm around. He'll know something weird is going on in his head. All I'm picking up from his surface emotions is an eagerness to get to where he's going.

We tried so hard to keep our chill. The squirrel used a combination of trees and rooftops to travel above the street wherever he could—wait.

<Atticus, is this squirrel a dude?>

Yes.

<What's his name?>

Squirrels don't have names that translate well into English. I mean, you're not going to find a Bob or a Jacob or a Zachariah. They use a gender pronoun followed by an accomplishment or an embarrassment, and sometimes they change. Right now this one is called He-Who-Knows-How-To-Travel-On-Loud-Shiny-Human-Tube-Things. Trains, in other words.

<That's actually encouraging. It means not all the squirrels have figured it out yet.>

We kept after him and gradually realized that we were in familiar territory: he was leading us to Washington Park.

<Hey, are we headed back to the Japanese Gardens?> Orlaith asked.

We're headed in that general direction. But Washington Park is pretty big.

<It's a trap!> I said in my best impression of Admiral Ackbar.

It's probably completely innocent, Oberon. There's an arboretum in there, remember? That means it will have some nuts and seeds a squirrel can't find anywhere else in Oregon. He's probably interested in gourmet nuts and is willing to travel for them.

<I don't know, Atticus. I've never heard of any nuts worth this much trouble. But we'll wait and see, as you said.>

It turned out not to be, as Atticus insisted, completely innocent. It wasn't even a little bit innocent. The squirrel didn't lead us to the Japanese Gardens or the arboretum, but rather to what I can only call a Dread Assemblage. I can count to twenty just fine, and there were more than twenty trees in a wooded area of the park that had more than twenty squirrels each in them! He-Who-Knows-How-To-Travel-On-Loud-Shiny-Human-Tube-Things scrambled up one of the trees and Atticus said this was where he wanted to go, so we could go ahead and bark all we wanted. The thing is, we were too stunned to let rip more than a confused woof or two. We'd never seen so many squirrels in once place before and didn't know what to do. They were chattering away but not fighting over anything. They were obviously there to cooperate on something, a conspiracy right under our noses—or above our noses, since they were all sticking to the branches out of our reach. That's when I counted them.

<Atticus, what's twenty times twenty?>

Four hundred.

<That's more than a million, right?>

No, it's far less.

<Well, it doesn't matter! The number of squirrels we have here is clearly unsafe!>

I don't feel particularly endangered.

Starbuck must have felt encouraged by that somehow because he started barking in earnest, leaping up to scare the squirrels if he could. They chattered back at him, probably making fun, but didn't move around or seem very worried.

Orlaith said, <You'd admit this is weird, though, right?>

Oh, sure, I've never seen this before. It's pretty cool.

I spluttered, <Cool? How can you say that, Atticus?>

I like it whenever I see something new. Gaia always finds a way to surprise me somehow, and I think it's wonderful.

<No, no, no, none of that! Find out why they're here and then we'll see how wonderful it is. Go on, ask that one who was on the train.>

Okay, I will. There was a pause and Atticus had this tiny little grin on his face like everything was so amusing and there was nothing to worry about. But I kept watching his face and when the grin fell away and turned into a frown, I asked him what he found out. *Uh, well. It's pretty disturbing.*

<I can handle the truth!>

They're here to discuss how to deal with you. Well, not you specifically, but dogs in general. They think you're annoying.

<Ha! That takes a lot of nerve, calling us annoying!> Orlaith said.

<Yeah!>

It gets worse. They think the best way to get rid of dogs is to get rid of humans, which they think will be easier for some reason.

<Oh, well, they can dream on! If bears couldn't do that, what chance do they have?>

That's what they're here to talk about. But uh, Starbuck is kind of making their point right now. Starbuck?

My little Boston buddy was still barking at the Dread Assemblage and they'd all stopped chattering except for one. He was in the tree above Starbuck, and he pointed one of his little paws straight at Atticus. As one, four hundred squirrels all turned to look at my Druid, and I knew what they were thinking: Get rid of one human and you get rid of all his dogs.

Starbuck, stop. I think we should go. Really. Oberon, Orlaith, let's go get that poutine. Atticus started backing away, and I was just about to argue with him when that one squirrel screeched and then all the squirrels started scampering down their trees. It's a mighty creepy thing, hearing all those claws scrabbling on tree bark, seeing all those fluffy tails twitching, all those dead black eyes coming right at you.

<Gah! It really is a trap! We can't repel squirrel power of that magnitude!>

Let's take a strategic lunch break right now, Atticus said. *Fast. Come on, run!*

I had to run through the streets of Cairo once with Atticus while all the cats of that city chased us right into the Nile river, and I remember feeling humiliated by it, hoping nobody was filming it to put on YouTube later. This was worse. But different, too: Once we got to the boundary of the park, the squirrels stopped chasing us. And it was also different because Atticus was laughing about it, clutching his stomach because he could hardly breathe.

<What are you doing? That wasn't funny!> I said.

Are you kidding? That was the most fun I've had in ages! Whoo! What a trip! Running for my life from four hundred squirrels! Know how many times I've done that in two thousand years? Just this once. That's a rare day for you.

<Atticus, we've just uncovered a vast conspiracy and you're ignoring it!>

Nah, I understand, Oberon. I get it now. Squirrels are dangerous.

<Finally!> Orlaith said.

<You *say* that, but you're still smiling.>

I'm going to be smiling for days and you'll just have to deal with my joy. But I also know we must be vigilant—and we will! But the squirrels are just talking. They won't start anything today. It's safe to go get lunch and enjoy the rest of the city. Who's hungry?

I didn't trust the expression on Atticus's face. He was trying to change the subject to food and I've been with him long enough now to know that when he does that he's trying to hide something. He probably didn't share everything he found out from the super tiny mind of He-Who-Knows-How-To-Travel-On-Loud-Shiny-Human-Tube-Things. Orlaith and Starbuck weren't used to such shenanigans, though.

<Yes food!> the Boston said.

<I'm ready,> Orlaith agreed. <If we're going to defend all humanity from the coming squirrel menace, we should have some gravy first.>

Well, I couldn't argue with her reasoning there. She's a super smart hound, and *I'm* a super lucky one.